TRENCH RAIDERS
By Sean McLachlan

For Almudena, my wife

And Julián, my son

CHAPTER ONE

13 September 1914

This valley looked like trouble.

Major Neville Thompson squinted through a cold rain out across the broad river valley. It was about a mile wide with a steep slope on the south bank where he stood, and an even steeper one on the north. Both lengths of high ground stood perhaps 300 feet above the valley floor. The slopes were mostly covered by forest, broken here and there by farmhouses and a few villages the Germans hadn't had time to burn.

The valley bottom was more open and exposed. Through the center meandered the Aisne River, yet another obstacle on the road to Berlin, except this looked to be a bigger obstacle than most. The bridges had all been blown and the river, while only about as wide as the Isis at Oxford, looked deep and unfordable. A series of large villages stood along its banks.

On the far slope, white puffs of artillery fire told him the Germans had decided to make a stand. The ridge the Germans held had several spurs that probed like fingers almost to the river's edge. Getting across the river and up that slope in the face of those guns, crossfire from the spurs, and surely a few other nasty surprises, would not be a carnival ride.

Well, nothing to do but try.

Major Thompson limped along a muddy stretch of French road that led into the valley. The sheeting rain lashed at his face as he watched his company march into battle. They were soaked to the skin, more asleep than awake from weeks of hard marching and fighting, but they slogged through the mire with a grim determination.

They were also outpacing him and putting him in danger of being left behind.

Thompson had one arm around Sergeant-Major Thomas Cole's shoulder. Cole was a head shorter than Thompson and made the perfect crutch. He had also turned out to be a good second-in-command after Captain Briggs had his head blown off at Mons.

"This is absurd," Thompson grumbled as he tried not to put any weight on his sprained ankle. "Two weeks under fire and I'm put out of commission by a shell hole."

"Oh now sir, don't you trouble yourself about it. At least the weather hasn't turned cold enough to snow," Cole replied.

"Snow would be a blessing. It would harden up these roads. The men are exhausted."

It had been a miserable two weeks of retreat as the Germans pushed into France. Retreat, skirmish, retreat, skirmish, retreat, all the while leaving poor wounded boys behind for lack of transport. Then, three days ago near the Marne, a miracle. It turned out the Germans were as worn out as they. The enemy blundered by separating their forces when they were almost within sight of Paris. The French and British counterattacked and the Germans withdrew in panic, or so the High Command said.

Thompson wished it had been panic. The Germans had fought a stubborn rearguard action for the last hundred miles. That meant more losses for his company.

This time the men could accept them. No one would ever forget the feeling that blessed morning when they received orders to move north instead of south. Worn out legs suddenly gained new strength, packs didn't seem so heavy, and everyone was eager to push on to Berlin. To die now would at least mean something.

Thompson hobbled along, leaning on Cole, who took most of his commander's weight while still carrying his pack and rifle. To their right was a pasture, where amid the churned up mud and droppings lay the butchered remains of a cow, reduced to a cavernous arch of ribs, a mess of offal, four splayed stripped legs, and a head that looked almost ludicrous in its perfect preservation and placid, stupid stare into nothingness.

To the left spread an open field of trampled wheat. At the center was a Royal Army Medical Corps wagon. A pair of medical orderlies treated three British soldiers lying on stretchers, probably wounded in that crackle of gunfire Thompson had heard half an hour before. On a groundsheet beside them sat the slumped figures of a half-dozen German wounded, bandages around heads or arms, left behind by their retreating army.

Sergeant-Major Cole tut-tutted.

"Well, they've certainly been given sore treatment, sir. Doesn't seem fair, sir."

"We had to leave many of our men behind these past days," Thompson said.

"Yes, but look! Not a Bosche among the medical lads. We always left someone with our wounded."

Thompson saw Cole was right. Cole noticed a great deal, which is why Thompson thanked his stars he had reenlisted.

"Yes, well I daresay we will be getting our own fellows back soon enough."

"Shall we stop and get your ankle wrapped, sir?"

"No, they have real wounded to treat. I'll put it up when we stop for the night. A few hours off it and I'll be right as r—"

The two men glanced up at the rain splattering their faces. Both chuckled.

"Well in any case I'll be on the mend," Thompson laughed.

Cole edged Thompson further to the side of the road as a pair of horses slogged past drawing a wagon, not military issue but obviously some farmer's pride and joy requisitioned for the duration. It was filled with worn-out men of the 2/4 Oxfordshire and Buckinghamshire, including several from Thompson's E Company. Some lay prone. Others sat slumped and rocking from side to side with the jouncing of the wagon. In the weeks of constant marching and foul weather, many strong young men had collapsed. Thompson, at 42, would have broken down long before if he hadn't had a horse much of the time.

"You hurt your ankle, sir?" a young man sitting on the back of the wagon said. He had his boots off and his feet, exposed to the pelting rain, were blistered and bloody.

"Yes, Corporal Willoughby," Thompson snapped.

The wagon was already pulling ahead. Willoughby called over his shoulder to the driver. "Hello, James! Stop for a moment, if you please."

The wagon pulled to a halt and Willoughby put on first one, then the other sock, wincing as the wool rubbed against his sores.

"It's best if you ride, sir. I can walk," Willoughby said.

"I'm quite all right, corporal."

"You are far more essential to operations than—ah!"—Willoughby's sentence was interrupted with a cry of pain as he pulled on one boot—"than I, sir. I'll walk."

"Corporal, I—"

"I think it's for the best, sir," Cole said. "We need you fresh, sir."

Thompson bit his lip, studied the wagon, and with a snarl mounted onto Willoughby's place as the corporal eased himself off. For a moment Thompson and Cole watched as Willoughby hobbled along the road, using his rifle as a crutch and not even attempting to match the pace of the rest of the battalion.

"Cole," Thompson said, turning back to him.

"Yes, sir."

"That's Hugh Willoughby, I know his parents slightly. Was in the Oxford University Reserves when he was called up. A good boy and fluent in French and German."

"Well, he certainly should be of some use, sir."

Cole needed no further instruction. He hurried to catch up with Willoughby—a task that took all of a few seconds—spoke softly with the youth for a moment, and relieved the boy of his pack. Cole loosened the straps, balanced the pack on top of his own, and wrapped the straps around his own pack and under his arms. The two set out, Cole looking like an ant carrying an oversized crumb, Willoughby walking like an old man with a young face. Thompson nodded in appreciation.

The major turned his attention to the men passing by in column. They were drenched, hungry, tired, footsore, but they had a set to their gaze that hadn't been there a few days before. Even their pace had quickened now that they were chasing instead of being chased. Thompson felt a deep embarrassment to be sitting on the back of this wagon, but Cole and Willoughby were right. He'd be no good to his men if he couldn't stand on his own two feet when they finally caught up to the enemy.

And when would that be? Were the Germans really making a stand or engaging in just another delaying action? The roadside was littered with evidence of their passing—broken down wagons, dead horses, discarded equipment, and a scattering of empty wine bottles that had obviously been liberated in much the same fashion as the wagon on which he rode. And then there were the burnt villages and farms. Few buildings had been left standing; even the outhouses had been torched.

But of the Germans themselves they had seen little. Daily skirmishes that never amounted to anything but delaying the British advance an hour or two, and a few firm stands while German engineers blew bridges or train trestles. Other than that, the Germans had been content to withdraw almost as quickly as they had once advanced.

"Surely they plan to make a stand somewhere," Thompson muttered. "Perhaps this is the place. If they're organized enough, they'd be fools not to stop here."

"Pardon, sir?" the slumped man sitting next to him asked. Thompson couldn't remember his name.

"The Germans. They must be planning to make a stand."

The private looked around.

"It does look like they legged it through this part, sir."

Thompson nodded. Most of the buildings here remained intact. There were even a few civilians about. Some were fleeing, pushing handcarts full of their possessions, while others stayed inside and peeked out of the windows. From what he could see of the villages along the river, they looked intact as well.

"Probably in a hurry to blow the bridges and get settled on the north bank," Thompson said.

"Oh, sir, I think they've had enough. Once they saw us coming they knew they were done in and decided to go home."

Thompson smiled. Such optimism was healthy, especially after all they had been through, but it wasn't realistic.

He reached into his pocket and pulled out a map of France. Hunching over to keep it out of the rain as much as possible, he opened it. The soldier leaned over a bit and looked. When Thompson glanced at him the soldier looked away and sat up straight.

"We are about here," Thompson said, pointing to a spot about a hundred miles northeast of Paris.

"Where's the road, sir?" the private asked, leaning in again.

"It's too small. It's not on here," Thompson grumbled. Neither was the village they had just passed through or much of the important topography. The map had been torn out of a *Baekdeker's* guide. Real maps were in short supply and he wasn't of sufficient rank to be graced with one.

"Now as far as I can tell the best place to make a stand would be at this river."

"That seems right, sir."

Thompson liked engaging his men in this manner, although many of his fellow officers sneered at the practice. If the men were better aware of the overall nature of the campaign, he reasoned, they could fight more intelligently. He only wished he himself was better aware of what was going on. The higher command hadn't seen fit to tell him anything except the day's orders, which consisted of: "Reveille, 0330; Parade, 0400; Breakfast, 0430; March 0530." After that it was "March" until told to stop.

A distant boom thudded from the north.

"That sounded like the Bosche blowing another bridge, sir," the private said.

Thompson perked up. There were two more booms in rapid succession.

"No, they've already done that. That sounds more like one or two of their 15 centimeter guns," the major said. "They haven't used anything that heavy on us for some time."

"You're right, sir. It's been all field guns, and not many of those."

Several more booms echoed across the valley, sounding strangely muffled yet more resonant because of the rain. The tired men of the column began to look up from their feet and peer curiously in that direction. More puffs of smoke lifted from the north bank of the River Aisne. Thompson wondered what British units were down in the valley getting shelled, but no one had seen fit to tell him that either.

Thompson went back to studying his map, which was rapidly getting soaked no matter how much he tried to protect it.

Just then a staff car came honking through the column, the men parting like a grumbling sea of khaki. Thompson's battalion commander, Lieutenant-Colonel Nesbitt, rode in the back. Some of his staff sat with him and a few of the other majors and captains trotted behind on their horses.

"Ah, Thompson, there you are!" Nesbitt motioned to him with his swagger stick.

Flushed with embarrassment, he saluted.

"I heard your horse was shot, bad luck. We'll have to see about getting you a suitable replacement."

Thompson hopped off the wagon and went over to the staff car with an exaggerated limp.

"You're wounded, Thompson?"

"It's minor, sir. I'm still fit to fight."

"Good show. Hop in. We can't have you riding in the back of a cart. I've heard about your soft touch with the men. That's all well and good but there are limits, my good fellow."

As one of Nesbitt's staff begrudgingly gave him room, Thompson sat down.

"We're collecting everyone for a staff meeting," his commander explained. "There's a village up ahead where we're setting up. It looks like the Germans have finally decided to make a bit of a stand. You say you're fit to fight, well, fight you shall."

With a rev of the engine and a honk of the horn, the car sped down the lane.

"Ah, the famous Company E!" Lieutenant-Colonel Nesbitt said expansively. "We have a bit of a wager about you at Brigade HQ. So tell me, just how did the Oxs and Bucks manage to come out a company extra?"

"If I understand it, sir, I believe the Brigadier said it was a clerical error. By the time it was discovered it was too late to demobilize, sir."

"A clerical error, indeed! Although I must admit to being perfectly content to have an extra 227 men."

"It's now 215, sir."

Nesbitt's face darkened a moment.

"Yes, a bloody business this is, Thompson, bloody business. And from what the aeronautic scouts tell us, it is about to get a good deal bloodier."

CHAPTER TWO

Private Peter Saunders hummed a tune as he marched through the rain. To be sure, he had never felt so tired in his life, and after just a few hours of waterlogged sleep they'd been awoken at an ungodly hour to march toward the sound of guns through a frigid deluge that soaked his toes from where they stuck out of the front of his ruined boots. Still, the fact that they were marching forward, not backward, made all the difference. The Bosche were on the retreat and after another few miserable weeks they'd be in Berlin and it would all be over. He'd see Candice and little Annabelle for Christmas.

That thought gave energy to his legs as he slogged with the rest of the Oxfordshire and Buckinghamshire boys along yet another muddy, rainy French road. Everyone grumbled about the rain and the mud just like they had grumbled about the heat and the dust until the weather had turned a week ago, but for Saunders that wasn't the worst part of the war. No, not the weather or the bad food or the constant marching or even the bit about getting shot at.

The worst part of the war was the smell. He hadn't had a bath in more than a week. He stank. The whole company stank. The whole army stank. Thousands of stinking, unshaven men marching along in close formation. Add to that the bloated corpses by the side of the road and you had a stench worse than cousin Jimmy's tannery.

Saunders had hoped that the rain would get rid of the smell; instead it had taken the reek of stale sweat and unwashed armpits and turned it into a musty funk that was even worse.

He could imagine what it would be like coming home to Candice and Annabelle like this. It would be like a moving picture. There he'd stride onto the screen as the piano player did a cheery rendition of "Rule Britannia". The grainy black-and-white Saunders would pose and strut all fine in his uniform, preen himself a little, and knock on his own front door. Maybe the piano player would pound on the side of his piano in time to his knocking, *clunk clunk clunk,* just like that bloke who worked at the Bicester Playhouse did sometimes.

Then the piano player would switch to "Home Sweet Home" as Candice opened the door and flung her arms wide to greet her hero back from the war. They'd fly toward one another, ready to embrace, but at the last moment Candice would swoon, wave her hand in front of her face, and run back inside.

Saunders would scratch his head and look bewilderedly at the audience as they laughed at his expense. Then little Annabelle would come out, ready to leap into Da's arms. She'd make a face, hold her nose, and flee into the house after her mother.

Saunders would look at the audience distraught, and a moment later Candice would reappear with the washtub in her hands. To riotous applause from the audience, she'd douse him with soapy water. The End. On to the next item in the program.

Yes, I'll certainly have to find a bathhouse in Berlin once this is all done with. I wonder if the Germans bathe?

He had to get there first, and that meant a few hundred more miles of marching. There was nothing to see along the road but the usual mess, so he focused on putting one foot in front of the other and let his thoughts wander to Christmas.

What should he buy them for presents? Well, he supposed he'd get to stop in Paris on the way back. He could buy Candice some nice French cloth to make a dress. A lot of the wives would be getting that. She'd be in fashion! Annabelle would get a pretty little French doll. At three she didn't know the difference between a French doll and an English one, but she'd be happy to sit on her Da's lap next to the Christmas tree and get a gift.

"Five minute's rest!" Sergeant-Major Cole's voice rang down the line.

Amid sighs and groans, the column moved to the side of the road and squished down in a meadow. Several of the men took a few further steps, dropped their drawers, and squatted. Saunders wrinkled his nose. Diarrhea had hit the battalion hard. Too much drinking from streams next to well-manured fields. Saunders moved upwind. As he sat down on the wet grass, he broke out some biscuits and watched the Royal Artillery wagons drawing some 18-pounder field pieces up the road, great clots of mud shearing off their wagon wheels.

"Good to see those going up," Saunders said. "They'll send the Hun scampering soon enough."

"Won't reach," mumbled Private Timothy Crawford from around a biscuit he was munching as he sat next to Saunders.

"What do you mean?"

"Won't reach. Those popguns don't have the range to hit the top of that ridge."

"Nonsense!" Saunders said. Crawford was one of the biggest grumblers of the bunch. Good man in a fight, though.

"My brother is in the Royal Artillery," Crawford insisted. "He's told me a thing or two."

"Is he is with that lot?"

Crawford shook his head. "The Devil knows where he is right now. But I don't need him here to tell me those guns can't reach."

"Ah well, the 60-pounders will reach, surely," Saunders said cheerily.

Crawford looked at him. "When's the last time you saw a 60-pounder?"

"Why, just yest—well, maybe the day before yesterday. No, it might have been a day or two before that."

Saunders lapsed into silence. He pulled out a photograph from his inside pocket and, hunching over to protect it from the rain, studied the faces of Candice and Annabelle. It was a fine snap of all three of them together, he in his uniform, sitting with Annabelle on his lap, and Candice standing behind him with a hand on his shoulder.

"Be back soon," he whispered. He saw Crawford glance at him but didn't notice his expression. He didn't want to know and didn't care.

Crawford was trouble, and in the army trouble had a habit of catching as quick as a cold.

A series of booms up ahead told him he'd be catching some trouble soon enough. Even from where he sat he could see the white puffs of artillery fire rising to mingle with the low gray clouds.

"Form column!" Sergeant-Major Cole's voice rang out again.

The men groaned and grumbled as they got to their feet.

"Look lively lads," Saunders said. "Berlin by October and Oxfordshire by Christmas!"

A few men cheered. Others managed a tired smile. Crawford did not cheer or smile.

Getting down to the valley bottom took much of the morning. The road was clogged with men and wagons. One of the artillery pieces had overturned and caused a blockage. At one corner of the snarled intersection, a harried medical detachment was transforming a large chateau into a hospital and already welcoming its first guests. A German artillery shell screamed overhead and shattered a tree in the chateau's garden.

The head surgeon, his smock bespattered with blood, stormed out the front door, strode across the manicured front lawn to the overturned gun and the men trying to right it, pointed down the road in the direction of Berlin and shouted,

"That way! Make the war go that way! Can't you see I'm busy here? My wagons need to get through!"

With that he stomped back to the chateau as the Tommies at the gun stared at him. A bawl from their sergeant made them put their shoulders to the frame and push. The gun gave a bit, but didn't become unstuck. They borrowed a horse from another team, hitched it to the gun mount, and with a snap of the whip and a pawing at the mud, yanked the gun out of the mud and onto the firmer land of the chateau's front lawn. It painted a pair of muddy tracks in a large semicircle on the grass before it was reunited with its team and taken back into the column.

The men quickstepped around it the next time they came to open fields. Saunders gritted his teeth at the feel of the fast pace after so many hours, so many weeks.

But they were free of the delay and going forward. The road led steeply down before almost flattening out at the edge of the valley bottom. The land opened up into pastures and farmhouses, dull green and gray in the rain. One of the farmhouses had its roof caved in from a shell. As they marched fully into the open, Saunders glancing over his shoulder and seeing the whole of the Oxs and Bucks behind him, an artillery shell landed with a crump in a field not two hundred yards away.

While nobody flinched, bitter experience made everyone curl in on themselves as they marched, keeping their heads low. A minute later another shell landed, further away this time, and Saunders breathed a little easier as he saw the next stretch of woodland come up.

They found it to be a mixture of orchards and wild growth surrounding a village made up of a dozen or so large stone farmhouses. One building's wall had a hole the size of man knocked out of it. An 18-pounder now took up the space, the crew firing with its barrel angled at 45 degrees. The shells landed halfway up the slope, well below the German guns.

Saunders was nearly six feet tall, and could look over shoulders of the few rows of men marching ahead of him. Craning his neck first one way and then the other, he could get a good look at what was coming up. The road out of the village widened and became flat and cobbled. Beyond lay the river and over it a bridge. The steel suspension made it halfway across the water before disappearing into a crumpled ruin, only to come back to life twenty feet beyond in a section of almost identical length as the first, still firmly attached to the north shore.

"Single file!" Major Thompson shouted.

There was some shuffling about and bumping by men who should have been in bed instead of marching into enemy fire, but within five steps the column had resolved itself into a single neat column.

"Slow march!"

After another minute Saunders found out why.

Spanning the space between the bridge sections was a single wooden board. Men were going across single file. Major Thompson stood on the other side and the front of the column was just now stepping off the bridge. On the river to the left the Royal Engineers were building a pontoon bridge while further on several rowboats ferried men across. Then it was Saunders' turn on the board and he had eyes only for that.

A glance down banished any thought of a second look. He focused on the board ahead, allowing his vision to blur out the appalling reach of empty air below.

Silence fell over him like a heavy blanket. Everyone in the column stopped talking, or if they did talk he was too focused to hear them. Nor did any German shells land. If they did he was a goner. The board was certainly wide enough, and felt sturdy even though there must have been four men on it at any one time, but he felt a bit as if he were on advertisement. Anyone within a mile could see him.

The shriek of a German shell. Saunders couldn't help but take an awkward half step when the shell landed in the river with a whoosh and a column of foam. The air, and the wood beneath his feet, reverberated with the sound.

Saunders felt a spike of fear for the moment it took to stop wobbling, right himself, and resume his pace. His nerves burned with white heat for the few steps it took him to make it to the bridge and then the sweet safe familiar mud beyond.

"Berlin by October, Paris in November, Oxford for Christmas," Saunders reassured himself.

CHAPTER THREE

Major Thompson cursed under his breath as he led his men through the woods. His ankle still pained him despite a rest in the staff car and having his ankle wrapped by Lt.-Col. Nesbitt's medical orderly. It did no good for the men to see him limping.

The 215 men of Thompson's E Company had been sent ahead of the rest of the battalion. They were to join up to the end of the British right, where they would reinforce the Second Connaught Rangers and secure the link with the French Seventh Army to the right of them. From what Nesbitt had told him that morning, the French were on their left too, their First Army being about 15 miles down the line at the other end of the British Expeditionary Force. It looked like the big show.

He glanced around him. The Lt.-Col. had said the third hill on the right from the last farmhouse, but there had been that little hump, hardly worthy of being called a hill. Did that count or not? He guessed it did. Better to go too short than too far. Wouldn't want to come up behind the French. They got a little panicky when they saw anything other than a blue field coat and red trousers. And in this rain, you didn't have to be terribly far away before it became difficult to tell German gray from British khaki.

Those red trousers show up all too well in the rain, Thompson mused. *I wonder if Joffre will cut his losses and arrange a change of attire.*

Wheeling his men left, he led them uphill. The slope was steep and made slick from the rain. Once he slipped on the wet grass and turned his ankle, wincing with pain. He glanced at Cole, saw he hadn't noticed, and kept going.

"At least that hot spell broke, sir," Cole said, squinting out from under his dripping field cap. He moved slightly closer, and Thompson realized that he had seen his look of pain after all and was waiting to catch him if he fell again.

"The men weren't accustomed to it," Thompson replied, embarrassed. "Nor I, I'm afraid. I haven't felt that lathered since the Transvaal."

"If memory serves, sir, the veldt was far worse."

"At least the Germans aren't as good shots as the Boers," Thompson grunted.

"No, sir, this won't take three years like South Africa did, thank God."

An artillery shell banged up ahead in a flash of red and a blossom of smoke. The gunfire grew louder.

"Column, halt! Cole, take a section forward and see where we are."

Cole did as he was ordered and returned a few minutes later saying they'd come up short. Apparently that half-hill hadn't counted as a hill after all. Thompson grumbled, limped with his men further along the slope, and then moved up.

The rain continued in a nonstop drizzle. That and the close-set trees and underbrush kept visibility down. Although Cole assured him the line lay barely a thousand yards up slope, Thompson couldn't see a single man. Another shell exploded, closer this time, and they began to come across wounded staggering back toward the rear, or sitting dazed beneath the trees. One man lay in a bloody ruin, his arm and half his chest torn off by a shell.

A bullet hummed a few inches over Thompson's head. He resisted the urge to duck. Limping in front of the men was bad enough. Through the trees he caught sight of a ragged line of soldiers in khaki lying behind trees and rocks and firing uphill.

"Everyone down!" he ordered. "Crawl forward."

He glanced at Cole and saw his old companion look relieved. Thompson smiled. Some officers thought it very dash to march boldly into combat. Three years chasing Boer guerrillas over terrain of their own choosing had taught him the ridiculousness of any such posturing.

As they wormed their way uphill, Thompson grateful all the while for not having to put weight on his ankle, a group of officers waved to them from behind a cluster of rocks. Thompson ordered his men to halt. He and Cole crawled to the officers.

"Major Sarsfield of the Connaught Rangers," the lead officer said, saluting. His upper class accent showed he was Anglo-Irish, unlike his men, who spoke in brogue so thick Thompson had to reassure himself they were speaking his language. "You Thompson?"

Thompson returned his salute. "Yes I am. What's the plan?"

"I've heard good things about you, Thompson. Now that you lads are here Nesbitt wants us to push the Huns over this ridge. They're entrenched about a thousand yards up, with some field guns a bit beyond that. Our guns can't reach this high from across the river and you've seen the state of the bridge. We won't have artillery support until the pontoon bridge is finished, and that will be hours. By then the Hun will have improved his defenses."

"Will the French be helping?" Thompson asked, peering through the trees in a vain attempt to spot the French position.

"They've been pressing hard all morning to no effect. I'll wager that the Huns have most of their men facing them, so if we hit hard now we can punch through. Form your men up over there, open order. Nesbitt wants us to take the German trench at bayonet point."

The two Majors saluted each other. Thompson and Cole withdrew. As they parted Thompson realized that they hadn't determined who had seniority. Not that it mattered at the moment. Nesbitt's orders had been clear enough.

The company fixed bayonets and spread out. Cole ran up and down the line getting the men in order. Once in position, they crept up and joined the line of the Irishmen.

"'Bout fucking time ya got here," one of the Irish soldiers muttered as they shifted left to give Thompson's company room on the far right of the British line. A thicket running down the slope to their right separated them from the French. Steady gunfire coming from that direction told him they were busy.

Major Sarsfield blew a blast on his whistle. Thompson rose to his feet, Webley revolver in one hand and sword in the other, and waved his men on.

For the first three hundred yards they advanced at a full run, eager to gain as much ground as quickly as possible. Thompson tried to ignore the pain in his ankle. There was a sputtering of gunfire but the Germans could see as little as the British. As they drew closer, however, the spiked tops of the German *Pickelhaube* came into view from their shallow trench, a serrated line cutting across the slope.

Flares from muzzle blasts illuminated the line. A Maxim gun opened up a little to the left, spitting bullets along the British formation. Several men fell.

"Down! Get down!" Thompson ordered.

"Get yer fucking heads down you cultchie snot bags!" bawled an Irish sergeant nearby.

The soldiers, both Irish and English, hit the dirt.

"Give them ten rounds rapid!" Thompson ordered.

The Tommies opened up. Trained for endless hours on the range to fire as quickly and as accurately as possible, they launched a hailstorm of bullets into the German lines. Several of the distant figures pitched over and fell. The rest put their heads down.

"Forward!"

The British line sprinted forward another twenty yards, Thompson gritting his teeth as pain lanced up his ankle with every step. The Maxim kept up its ceaseless drone, and the German riflemen regained their nerve and resumed fire. The man to the left of Thompson clutched his face and reeled back.

"Down!"

The British line hit the ground again, everyone squirming to get behind a tree or a rock or even the merest rise in the earth.

"Ten rounds rapid!"

The British fired again. Thompson could see that the Germans had cleared the undergrowth in front of their trenches. Cover for the advance would soon get scarce. Off to his left he could vaguely see the Irish banging away, but the smoke, trees, and the rain obscured his view. The Connaughts had gotten a little further ahead but the Maxim gun pushed them back until they ended up parallel with Thompson's line.

"Where are our machine guns?" Thompson wondered.

He scanned the woods behind, filled now with smoke and a few wounded writhing on the wet grass. He caught a glimpse of a man with a Red Cross armband helping a soldier with blood pouring down his face. He saw no sign of the machine guns.

"No good going against that position with no Vickers guns for support," he told Cole. "It's bad enough we have no artillery. Send a runner back to find out where they've gone and get them up here on the double!"

The British kept up a continuous fire, but it was an uneven contest. The Germans had dug in, and while the British hid behind trees and rocks, they were getting picked off one by one.

Then the German guns got their range.

A bang just overhead, followed by a ragged chorus of screams. Men twitched in pools of their own blood, torn apart by shrapnel. Another shell split a tree to the left and Thompson saw it plummet down and crush an Irishman.

"Where are those bally guns!" Thompson demanded.

As if in response, he saw his two machine gun crews emerge from the woods, bent almost double in the storm of fire and carrying the unwieldy Vickers guns between them.

Thompson positioned one on his extreme left to fire at the Maxim and support the Connaught Rangers, who seemed to be missing their own Vickers, and put the other in his center. They got into action within minutes. The guns raked the German line with deadly accuracy.

The Maxim was pummeled into silence, and any German who dared show his head was mown down.

"Forward!"

The Tommies charged forward a full hundred yards before the Germans had the nerve to fire back. As soon as they did, Thompson ordered his men down and his machine guns forward. After a few more casualties while the guns got set up, they repeated the whole maneuver, taking out more Germans and gaining another hundred yards.

At this point Thompson paused. They had a good view of the trenches now, and had proved that British rifle fire was superior to German, nullifying the Germans' better cover. Plus they had two Vickers machine guns to the enemy's lone Maxim. The German artillery fell silent. The English and Irish had gotten close enough that the gunners couldn't fire for fear of hitting their own trench. Yet Thompson paused.

"We daren't run through that open space," Thompson said.

"Didn't the gentleman say to take the position at the point of a bayonet, sir?" Cole asked.

Thompson looked at his old companion in disbelief. The fellow's aptitude for sarcastic deference was second to none.

"We keep up a good enough fire and we won't have to."

And so they did, for another brutal half hour as bullets flew in both directions. The fire from the German line slackened noticeably, the Maxim was knocked out by several lucky shots into its mechanism, and the enemy didn't seem to be getting reinforcements. Neither did the British, for that matter. Thompson wondered what was happening on his flanks but no message runners came and the din was such that he could hear nothing beyond what was close around him.

Thompson grew nervous. While they were giving more than getting, their position remained a hazardous one and casualties were mounting. With a flush of relief he saw two machine gunners bring forward fresh boxes of ammunition for the Vickers. His men must be getting low, however. They'd carried 150 rounds each up the hill, but rapid fire could drain that away in remarkably little time.

"How many rounds left per man do you think, Cole?"

"Might not matter, sir," Cole said, pointing at the German line.

The fire dribbled away. Thompson saw a white handkerchief being waved at the end of a Mauser. A cheer went up from the British line and soon all firing ceased. Through the rain they saw figures emerge from the trench, some with their hands up, some waving handkerchiefs, but many still carrying their rifles.

"Put your hands up!" Thompson called out.

"Hande hoch oder ich schiesse!" someone from the British line called out. Thompson recognized young Corporal Willoughby's voice.

That got a few of the Germans to oblige, but not all. More issued from the trench.

"That didn't take much," a Tommy laughed and stood up.

"Get back down!" Thompson ordered.

"Um, yes sir." The soldier looked confused.

All along the British line, men got up and sauntered toward the German trench.

"Hande hoch!" Willoughby shouted again. He had not risen.

"Get down, all of you!" Thompson shouted.

The Germans moved forward, still waving their handkerchiefs. More stepped out of their trench.

Despite Thompson's protestations, his line was disintegrating. Most had risen, some moving toward the Germans while others stood laughing with their comrades. The Irishmen closest to their left cheered and waved their caps. One man right next to Cole leapt up.

"Looks like we'll be in Berlin by week's end!" he laughed.

Cole grabbed him and hauled him to the ground.

"Get down, you bloody fool!"

Just then a line of Germans rose up in the trench and fired. A dozen Tommies jerked and fell, faces stunned, blood sprouting from mortal wounds. The Germans outside of the trench cringed and kept their hands up, or fell prone and started firing too.

CHAPTER FOUR

Captain George MacDonald, Royal Army Medical Corps, could not believe his eyes. He'd been tending the wounded a hundred yards behind the firing line when he saw the Germans raise the white flag. Once the firing stopped, he'd come up to tend to the wounded still in the line and liaise with the German medical staff.

Then the Germans had opened up on them. Dropped their own white flag and broke all conventions of civilized warfare. MacDonald had just enough time to duck behind a tree and save himself.

MacDonald peeked around the thick trunk and saw the British and Germans in a furious firefight at almost point-blank range. The hillside was littered with British casualties, but the Tommies had rallied quickly and Major Thompson had ordered rapid fire.

Not that they needed any encouragement. The men fired for all they were worth, snarling and cursing at the enemy. Those Germans outside the trench fell like ninepins, some still clutching their handkerchiefs ridiculously in the air. A few lucky ones leapt back in the trench, while their comrades who had never left the shelter fired down on the British.

A bullet plucked MacDonald's cap off his head, revealing his bald pate.

"Crikey!" MacDonald yelped, ducking back behind his tree.

A minute later he dared look again. The lines had gone back to their previous position. The Germans were all back in their trench or dead, and the Tommies were lying down along their firing line. Several wounded had been dragged back and each minute added to their number.

"Oh, bother. MacDonald old boy, it looks like you're needed."

Running low, he hurried up to the firing line and got to work on the first man he came to, a fellow who couldn't have been more than eighteen and whose knee had been shattered by a bullet. The soldier failed about on the ground, calling for his mother. MacDonald got to work. This boy would live if he clipped that artery quick enough, but he'd never walk again.

Once MacDonald finished with him, he moved to the next casualty, barely five yards from the first. This one was a head shot. The man was a goner so MacDonald placed a bandage on his head to keep up his friends' morale and moved to the next, a chest wound that looked salvageable.

An Irishman to the left stood up and blazed away at the German wounded who lay groaning between the lines.

"You fucking cunts!" *Bang.* "You don't raise a false white flag!" *Bang.* "Not even on Englishmen!" *Bang.*

MacDonald's work continued for what seemed like forever. Stretcher parties took away the wounded. To where, MacDonald didn't know. No one had bothered telling him where the dressing station was. As long as the stretcher parties knew, he was content. He'd need some supplies pretty soon, though.

The firing died down from a constant fusillade to a seething crackle. It was now afternoon and it was obvious the British weren't going to break through. The commander—Thompson, good chap, cared about the men—ordered a withdrawal back three hundred yards, leaving just a skirmish line to hold the ground that had cost them so dear.

After that the rifle fire died out almost completely. Every now and then the Germans sent a shell at them, but their artillery seemed to have shifted their focus to the valley floor. Not that MacDonald could really see. No one could see anything in these woods.

MacDonald organized a forward aid station just behind the new line. A couple of orderlies joined him. They did their best to keep the wounded comfortable until the stretcher bearers could take them down to the nearest village, where MacDonald hoped they'd get more treatment. The rain continued, and the wounded had to lie uncovered, their anguished faces blinking in the downpour. The weather had turned colder too. MacDonald shivered as the rain ran down his bare head.

A call came from their right.

"Hallo! Anglais!"

MacDonald and the others peered through the rain. Some of the men leveled their rifles.

Sergeant-Major Cole calmed them. "Don't get jumpy, lads."

A dark-faced man in a strange uniform emerged from the drizzle. He wore a blue and gold vest over loose white pantaloons tied with a red sash. On his head was a red fez. He had a narrow face, hooked nose, and black wooly hair.

"Anglais! Médecin? Au secours!" the newcomer said.

"He's an Arab!" one of the men said. "I've seen them in pictures."

"We have savages in front and on both sides," MacDonald said under his breath. "Fine position you're gotten yourself into MacDonald, old chap."

"Must be Moroccan," Willoughby said, and switched into French. *"Qu'est-ce qu'il y a?"*

The man gestured at MacDonald's Red Cross armband and made a long reply.

"He wants you to come see their wounded," Willoughby translated.

"What, haven't they medical staff of their own?" MacDonald asked.

Willoughby shrugged. "He's says they don't."

"Baker, Griffiths, you're with me," MacDonald called to two of the orderlies.

"Willoughby, go with them," Cole said.

Willoughby saluted. "Yes, sir."

The Moroccan led them along a steep slope, all of them having to go slowly as they slipped and slid on the wet grass. Soon they entered the thicket that separated the two lines. A few Oxfordshire men were stationed there, and as they moved through the closely set trees they came upon a group of Moroccans crouching in some brush and looking upslope.

MacDonald followed their gaze. One of the Irishmen had told him this thicket went up the slope all the way to the German lines. MacDonald's nerves grew taut at the thought of Germans hiding in the greenery, ready to shoot. The occasional bang of a field gun nearby told them the French were getting it as badly as the English were. The Moroccan kept hurrying ahead, turning and gesturing eagerly at the Englishmen lagging behind.

Willoughby was the worst straggler. MacDonald noticed that he walked with that awkward gait of a man who felt pain in both legs and was trying to favor neither one. It was an impossible task, so he used his rifle as a crutch and held onto any convenient branch as he made his painful way through the woods. MacDonald estimated that at least one man in ten had fallen out in the past week. Willoughby was obviously one of them, yet he still struggled to keep up.

The thicket was only about a hundred yards wide and soon they emerged to a clearer area beyond. The Moroccans had dug in a little up slope from where they came out of the woods. Their guide led them downhill a couple of hundred yards and into a large cave cut into the chalk hillside. Inside, a spirit lamp cast a feeble light. Lying on ground sheets were a score of Arabs clutching bloodstained rags to their wounds.

"Not a bandage in the lot," MacDonald said.

He frowned and turned to Baker and Griffiths. "Right then, let's get to work."

As the two orderlies began to clean wounds, MacDonald went around seeing how bad each man was. Two he could tell were hopeless cases. One had a nasty shrapnel wound to his chest. MacDonald gave him enough morphine to put him to sleep, knowing that he probably would be dead before he needed another injection. The other wound made MacDonald swear. The man had been shot in the arm. The bullet had pierced the main artery and blood soaked the Moroccan's vest and pantaloons and had spread in a wide pool around him. He was faint from loss of blood. An orderly could have dealt with this easily enough at the time, but now the man had bled out. MacDonald tied up the wound anyway, although the poor fellow was too weak to last the night.

The rest weren't much better off. None had received any care and some of the wounds looked a day old. All of them were soaked through from the rain and shivering in the cave's damp, cool interior. He didn't even see much evidence of food around.

Willoughby confirmed his suspicions. "They've been up here since noon yesterday. He says they've seen hard fighting ever since."

"When are they to be relieved?" MacDonald asked.

Willoughby translated the question. The Moroccan spread his hands and looked heavenwards. MacDonald grunted and got back to work.

"Willoughby, come here and help."

"I've never spoken with an Arab before," the young man said as he limped to the medical man's side. "His French is quite good, although with a strange accent that's almost—"

"Fascinating, I'm sure. Here, put direct pressure on this wound while I bandage it."

They worked nonstop for two hours. In that time the firing increased outside and they found themselves serving a whole new crop of wounded. During a lull MacDonald turned to Willoughby.

"Tell your heathen friend to send a message to his divisional officer requesting medical staff."

"He already complained about that to me, sir. He made that request yesterday, and twice today."

MacDonald looked around, biting his lip.

"We have to get back to our own division. Tell him I'll return tonight."

Looks like you're in for twice the work, MacDonald told himself.

They left the cave and skirted the lower end of a steep escarpment that covered them from fire. After a hundred yards the ground flattened to a gentle slope and they were soon very much out in the open. They ran low in single file, the Moroccan in the lead, Willoughby struggling just behind, followed by MacDonald and the two orderlies. All the Englishmen had drying blood on their hands.

A sudden storm of shots made them look uphill. The Germans had popped out from their trenches, half hidden by the intervening woods, and came down at the Moroccans in a rush. The Colonials blazed away. Germans fell every second, but they kept on and returned with a withering fire as they drew close.

Their guide turned and sprinted up the hill to join his mates. Willoughby glanced at MacDonald uncertainly. The doctor nodded and Willoughby struggled uphill, the obvious pain in his feet unable to dampen his eagerness to get into action.

The fight was hot but short. The Germans made a bold advance, firing all the way, but their marksmanship was mediocre and the Moroccans had dug in. When Germans started falling dead on other dead Germans, they backed off.

Willoughby and his friend came back with another casualty slung between them, a man with a chest puncture.

"There's a few more coming down behind us," Willoughby told him.

"We must get back," MacDonald said. He turned to Griffiths. "You stay here. Take my bag. I'll stock up back in the line."

MacDonald handed him his satchel containing his medicines.

Willoughby looked around, unsure.

"You need to get back to your unit," MacDonald told him. "Griffiths will just have to learn sign language."

They scampered through the thicket of woods and rough ground that cut downhill through both firing lines and the ground in between, and emerged on the far right of the Oxs and Bucks.

MacDonald knelt down by the first casualty he came to and got to work.

CHAPTER FIVE

14 September

Private Timothy Crawford crawled through a thick early morning mist, moving slowly and silently between the British and German positions. A night lying prone on the skirmish line had left his muscles stiff and his skin clammy. It felt good to be moving again.

Predawn light was just beginning to turn the black sky to gray and he wanted to get a good look at the Hun lines while he had the chance. Orders had been to stay on the skirmish line. Bugger orders. As soon as he could, Crawford had slipped away. It was time to go hunting.

But this was no poaching expedition near Rose Hill. These birds shot back. They stabbed in the back too. That trick they'd pulled yesterday was a damn bloody foul thing to do. Blackburn had copped it, and Ewing got a bullet in the hand that would cripple him for life.

He'd even the score before the sun rose.

The woods were eerily silent but for the occasional chirp of an early-rising sparrow. Moving on memory, he angled to the right, where he'd seen a dense copse at the far end of the Oxs and Bucks line. That would make good lookout post. For sure the Hun had a machine gun covering it, but in this soup they wouldn't be able to see what they were shooting at. Maxims were for mowing down masses of charging men, not for taking out a single sniper.

Crawford held his Short Magazine Lee-Enfield slightly above his shoulder to keep it off the grass and away from the dew. The SMILE, as everyone called it, was a good, sturdy weapon, but it paid to treat it with care. A little under 3 feet, 9 inches and weighing only 8 pounds, it felt made for sneaking around like this. Its ten-round magazine carried hefty .303 bullets that packed quite a punch and it was accurate right up the 2,000 yards for which it was sighted.

Not that he'd be firing at that range. He could barely see twenty yards, let alone two thousand.

A cluster of tall, dark shapes loomed up ahead. The copse. And none too soon, neither. The stretch he was crawling through was all but open, only the occasional tree adding cover to what, judging from the cow patties scattered here and there, the Frogs used as a pasture. The mist helped some, but he didn't want to be the lone shadow in this featureless field.

Ten yards from the copse he stopped and listened for a full minute. If he knew the spot made a good vantage point, it was a fair bet one or two of the smarter Huns would figure out the same thing.

If they were in there, they were keeping silent. The only way to find out was to go in and check.

A cough uphill made him freeze. The cough came again, with no attempt to suppress it. Obviously a Hun in the trench. No one creeping about would let himself make that much noise. The cough had sounded near, although mist did funny things with noise. Perhaps the trench was nearer than he remembered?

Taking extra care, he slid along the wet grass in a beeline for the copse, not caring that his path took him through some musty cow droppings. What's a little shit? He'd been neck deep in shit ever since the battalion disembarked in France.

Crawford came to the edge of the trees. Curling himself up behind the outermost one, he peered into the shrouded darkness. The field he had just left was a uniform pale gray and green thanks to the predawn light illuminating the mist. Inside the copse, however, little light penetrated and he could see barely ten yards in front of him.

He brought up his gun at a sudden scrabbling ahead. At the last instant he kept from squeezing the trigger. The scrabbling rose into the air before growing fainter and moving to his right.

Must be a squirrel. Crawford smiled.

He rose and entered the copse's nighted interior. Through gaps in the foliage a faint light filtered through in phantasmal beams, lending the palest gray to the mist. Deep shadows cloaked the space all around him. He placed each step with care, at times having to move his foot when he felt the slight resistance of a stick or pile of leaves under the sole of his boot. It wouldn't do to crawl through this mess. He'd wake up every Hun from here to Berlin. Plus there were his own men and the darkies strung out at the bottom of these woods. Wouldn't want them to shoot him in the back.

Crawford focused on keeping his position in his mind. He didn't know how thick the copse was, but he remembered the general lay of the enemy trench. He angled his course up slope and further into the copse.

After long, slow progress he saw a brightening up ahead, silhouetting the vague shadows of the last trees before the vegetation thinned out. Just beyond lay the German trench, although he still couldn't see it. He'd only been in the trees for perhaps ten minutes. The morning was brightening faster than he'd hoped. Were there clear skies above all this mist? That would be just his fucking luck. He'd cursed the rain for the past two weeks, they all had, but dark skies suited his purpose this morning.

Creeping to the edge of the copse, he could just make out a black line through the pale green ground. Within the line were several shadowy humps. Most had the telltale spike of the *Pickelhaube* helmet on top. The Huns. The other humps could be guns or equipment or Huns with their helmets off, although in this cold that last bit seemed unlikely.

Dotting the space in front of the trench were the round shadows of several tree stumps. The Huns had cleared the hillside for a few yards. Good thing they hadn't had time to clear more.

With the tree line this close to the trench the Huns would want a machine gun to stiffen things up. Where was it? That hump there? No, too small and no one next to it. Ah, there! Perhaps forty yards to his right stood an amorphous bulk flanked by a pair of spiked helmets. Forty yards? Damn, it really was getting brighter. Averting his eyes slightly to help his night vision, he could just discern that it was some bulky object nestled between piles of cut logs.

Splendid. The Hun had stolen some Frog's woodpile to protect their Maxim.

If only he had some sort of explosive to throw at that gun to blow it to bits. You'd think the Army would have issued such a thing. He'd heard of grenades but never seen one. Would one of those work?

No point in wondering. He didn't have one today and he wouldn't have one tomorrow. At least he could sort out the gun crew.

Positioning himself so that the muzzle flare would be behind a tree from the vantage point of the men in the trench directly opposite him, Crawford raised his rifle, aimed at one of the Maxim crew, exhaled slowly, and squeezed the trigger.

The gunshot cracked through the early morning air. A shadow cried out and toppled. Snicking back the bolt to eject the bullet and bring another into the chamber, Crawford fired less than two seconds later, not enough time for the other crewmember to shake off his shock and duck out of sight. Instead the Hun flew backwards, arms splayed, slamming against the back of the trench.

Crawford curled up at the base of the tree as Mausers erupted along the line. The fire was panicky, inaccurate. His trick of masking his muzzle flare from those closest to him had worked. It appeared none of the sleepy Germans had glimpsed his position.

"Feuer einstellen!" bawled a voice from the trenches.

The gunfire petered out. Crawford smiled.

Well, now I know how to say "cease fire" in Hunnish. This is becoming educational. I'll have to get that prat Willoughby to train me to say it right. Could come in handy.

The officer's voice had come from his left. Crawford eased his body to the right a bit so that his muzzle flash would once again be hidden by the tree from those directly to his front. He studied the shadows.

They were a lot shorter now. The Huns kept low in their trench, the spikes and domes of their helmets barely visible.

Which one was the officer? Impossible to tell. He had eight rounds left in his magazine. There was nothing for it but to give them rapid fire and hope he got the right one.

Crawford fired, racked back the bolt, fired again. Muzzle flashes lit up the German line. While those opposite him couldn't see his own flash, the rest of the Germans spotted it quick enough. Crawford didn't flinch as bullets snapped the air all around him. He racked the bolt, fired, racked it again, fired. Shadows tumbled and cried out. A bullet splintered the tree inches from his face. He racked the bolt again and made another shadow tumble.

He emptied his magazine, lay down between some thick roots, and took a five-round clip from his chest pouch. Using his thumb, he pushed the rounds into the top feed and tossed away the clip. He repeated the motion with another clip to fill the magazine.

The firing zeroed in on his position, bullets hacking off chunks from his tree. Best to move before firing again.

As he started crawling to his right, there came the rapid *tak tak tak* of the Maxim strafing the area.

Shit! They got their crew replaced quick enough!

The air filled with bits of bark and kicked-up dirt. Crawford lay prone until the storm passed, then crawled as quick as he could to get closer to the deadly machine gun. The Maxim made another sweep, cutting through the forest before concentrating on his former position.

Crawford found a sizeable rock about half as big as he was and hid behind it. The Maxim made another pass and Crawford listened carefully to judge where it was in relation to him. As the Maxim got to the point in its sweep furthest from his position, he popped up.

The flare of the Maxim's muzzle shimmered in the mist. He gave ten rounds rapid all around it and ducked back down.

The Huns fired back, but not with the Maxim.

Another goal for our side. Time to leg it.

Crawford snapped two more clips into the magazine and crawled down the slope. The darkness of the copse favored an easy retreat and soon he was far enough away that the bullets were going well wide. Still, he didn't dare stand up.

And that saved his life.

Over the din of gunfire he heard voices ahead. German, and too damn close.

Crawford froze. It sounded like two men having a hurried and hushed argument, no doubt wondering why their line had suddenly gone berserk.

The Huns sounded like they were just on the other side of a thick, mossy log that loomed in front of him like a low green wall. Crawford had gotten right up to them unseen. And unheard, thanks to the gunfire.

Crawford eased his Lee-Enfield into a ready position and moved his left knee forward. There was another burst of fire. Betting this would make the Germans put their heads down, Crawford rose to a kneeling position and leveled his rifle.

They lay barely five feet away. A pair of astonished faces stared at him like he was a ghost coming out of the night.

He shot one right between the eyes. Swiveling to hit the other one, he had his rifle batted to the side by the tip of the German's bayonet. His shot ploughed the earth.

The German whipped his bayonet back at Crawford's head, who had to fall backwards to keep from getting slashed in the face by the serrated blade.

Crawford fired again but the German dodged to the side. The man leapt over the log and drove his bayonet down at Crawford's chest. Crawford rolled away and leapt to his feet. The German lunged. Crawford jerked to the side as he felt a hot pain streak his ribs. He pumped a round straight into the German's gut.

After that it was all running. Crawford didn't want to hang about to see if more Germans were taking a stroll between the lines. His skirmish had launched a storm of metal into the copse and stealth was pointless. Once he got close to his own skirmish line he went prone and crawled back among his mates. One almost shot him on the way in.

Stuart James, Crawford's platoon sergeant, spotted him and bawled, "Crawford, where the blazes have you been?"

Crawford put on an innocent face.

"Went out to use the loo, sir. I hurried back when I heard the firing but I got turned around in the mist."

The sergeant's face turned red. He bellowed something else but Crawford couldn't hear the words, because at that moment the first of the German shells landed on the line.

CHAPTER SIX

Major Thompson was beginning to hate chalk. All night his men had been digging in, and as the morning mist began to glow with dim sunlight he saw their progress had been miserable. The standard issue entrenching tool was a tiny, flimsy thing. Most armies used a simple, short-handled spade. The British High Command, in its infinite wisdom, had designed a multipurpose tool. The shovel blade was stuck at right angles to the handle, with a miniscule pick on the back of the blade. Thus you couldn't dig with it properly, and it was too small to be a proper pick.

In soft English soil it worked well enough. In the dense chalk that underlay the few inches of topsoil on this slope it was nothing but an undersized garden hoe. The men had tried to use the pick end, but within the first five minutes one of the points had snapped off and nearly taken Thompson's eye out. They went back to using the shovels. Soon those were breaking too.

Many men took to using their bayonets. The best at it was Private Matthews, who had worked in an ice house in Abingdon. He chipped at the chalk in quick little lines, shearing off a blur of thin flakes. But even he didn't make much progress. He kept having to stop to sharpen his blade.

Thompson had watched all this through the night with increasing frustration until he lost his patience and joined in with his sword. Thompson's long service in the army had banished any illusions that the sword was a noble weapon. For three years he had hauled the wretched thing all around South Africa and while it proved effective against snakes, it was useless in battle. He soon discovered it was pretty much useless against chalk as well.

By morning the men barely had enough cover to lie down in, and were dead tired in addition. No hot food had come up and they had to make do with biscuits and water. Then some idiot started banging away at the Germans in the early morning hours and had gotten the enemy's wind up. After strafing a copse on the company's far right, the Germans followed up with an appallingly accurate artillery fire.

"Looks like they taped this entire slope, sir," Cole said. He was lying next to Thompson and still scraping away at the chalk with his bayonet.

Thompson checked his Webley revolver as well as the spare Lee-Enfield lying next to him. He'd gotten that off of one of the wounded, along with the webbing and ammunition pouches. He had a feeling he'd need it.

"Order the runners to bring up the unit ammunition reserve," Thompson ordered.

"Yes, sir. Philips, Coleman, Davies. Fetch the unit reserve!"

"This is a bad one. I think—" Thompson paused as another shell exploded "—they're preparing us for a charge."

"I suspect you are correct, sir," Cole said, chipping faster. His Lee-Enfield lay close at hand.

The cannonade increased in tempo, a regular *crack crack crack* as if of a giant bullwhip. The men squeezed into the shelters they had dug for themselves. A nearby hit whirred shrapnel over one section of the line, and three men who hadn't dug deep enough got sliced by it. One man was struck right through the head and died instantly. The other two gasped and held spurting limbs.

Thompson crawled to first one, then the other Vickers emplacements on either side of him to make sure they were ready. Finding the machine guns fully manned with plenty of ammunition and spare gunners lying a few yards behind, he returned to the center of the line next to Cole.

A messenger hurried up from the company's left.

"The Connaughts report movement to their front, sir."

Thompson and Cole spread word down the line to be ready.

The artillery fire lifted. A minute later it settled past their right, onto the French Colonial units. A request had come from them during the night for ammunition, but their Lebels took a different caliber and there was nothing Thompson could do. Judging from where the shells were hitting, it appeared the Moroccans still held the line. He hoped that would remain the case. He had put Sergeant James' platoon on the far right so Willoughby could act as liaison. He'd also sent MacDonald over there in the night to check on their wounded. Why he had to do the French divisional command's job was a question he'd very much like to have answered some time.

Oh, and he needed to fill out the paperwork to make Sergeant James' command of the platoon official. He had taken over after Subaltern Williams had been wounded last week. How many officers was he short now?

No time to worry about that. A few warning shouts rose from among his men. Thompson peered through the mist and drizzle. Shadows flitted through the dark lines of trees.

"At the ready!" Thompson shouted. "Wait for my order, then ten rounds rapid."

The vague, moving blots began to resolve themselves into individual silhouettes. They drew closer, yet remained indistinct because of the low light and the shadows of trees that stood scattered all along this slope. At times a German would be perfectly clear, then his form would meld into the dark line of a tree. Whether he was in front of or behind it was impossible to tell. Then once again he'd appear, only to disappear just as quickly.

"Hold your fire," Thompson warned.

The shadows drew closer. Thompson sensed a restlessness in his line.

"Hold it."

Suddenly the Germans weren't black shapes anymore, but men with faces and buttons and helmets and bayonets.

"Fire!"

Each man of the Oxs and Bucks gave the charging Germans ten rounds in less than a minute. Still the line came, slower, Germans falling or veering away, or going prone and firing, anything to avoid running full speed into that fire, yet most struggled on. More fell, then there was a panicked pause as Thompson's men cleared their magazines and had to thumb in more ammunition. The Germans rallied, those firing threw themselves to their feet and ran forward. Those already charging fired as they ran.

"Fire at will!" Thompson shouted.

The fastest Tommies were already ready, and in the following seconds more and more joined them. Once again lead pelted the closely packed German ranks. The charge slowed, staggered, held its ground for one uncertain second and then moved back. By the time the Oxs and Bucks had to reload again the withdrawal had become unstoppable. The attackers had lost too many.

Within ten minutes the British line was being hit by artillery again.

The shells only landed on their section of the line, sparing the Irish and the Moroccans. Runners coming back from the flanks told him why—the Germans were charging both.

"Probing for weak spots," Thompson said. "Let's hit them while they're busy elsewhere."

Cole and the sergeants spread the word. Everyone topped up their rifles and fixed bayonets. Waiting until there was a lull in the shelling, Thompson gave a blast on his whistle and the men sprang out of their shallow holes. It was still raining and the morning mist hadn't entirely cleared, so they made it halfway to the German line without getting fired upon. For a minute it seemed easy, the shells landed well behind them and the Germans ahead remained unaware of their advance.

That didn't last long. As the German trench resolved itself through the mist and rain a hundred Mausers flashed.

Men pitched over. Several of the British troops stopped and gave rapid fire into the trench. Others charged forward as fast as they could, eager to close, hoping that hand-to-hand combat would be safer than getting shot at out here in the open.

Just then the deadly rattle of a Maxim gun ripped the air, tearing through the British line. Thompson groaned. In the previous day's fight one of the Vickers had made a direct hit on the German machine gun and broke it. He'd seen that with his own eyes. The Germans had gotten themselves another.

"Back! Back!" Thompson cried.

Some of his men turn to him in wonder. The charge had barely begun. He admired their dash but knew it was futile. They didn't have the men to get through such fire. Soon everyone was withdrawing, only a few turning to give the Germans some rounds before taking flight back to the pitiful protection of their embryonic trench.

They barely made it before they saw the Germans come at them through the mist.

Now it was the Vickers' turn. Both guns tore through the German ranks. The front men fell and got replaced by the large host behind. Tommies swore as they hurried to reload, their magazines still depleted from the charge. The Germans drew closer, leaping over the mingled bodies of German and English, more filling up the mist behind, a horde of men, some firing, some falling, the crowd moving ever forward.

The attacking force heaved like a living thing. In front of the two Vickers guns it drew back and shifted to the sides. On both flanks it edged forward, approaching to within a stone's throw of the British line. Tommies started falling to their fire.

A harsh shout in a strange language sounded from the right flank, followed by a strange ululation that may or may not have been words. From the thicket that hemmed in the British right flank burst a hundred Moroccan troops. They hove into the Germans before the enemy fully realized they were there, gutting them with bayonets or clubbing them with rifle butts. Some had long, curved knives and leapt on the Germans, slashing throats, opening bellies.

The attack was so fierce, so sudden, the Germans barely had a chance to react. The infantrymen, trained for marching and firing, didn't know how to deal with this chaotic melee in which they found themselves. There were no lines, no single opponents. Arabs heaped onto lone Germans, while others whipped through whole crowds of the enemy, both fists gripping wickedly curved blades dripping gore.

Only one German, a big brute of a man, gave any sort of account of himself. Seeing his comrades getting slaughtered, he let out a roar and charged with his gun level, knocking down three Arabs before one was bold enough to stand in his way. He lanced this man in the chest, pulled out his bayonet with an audible pop and swung around to slash another Arab across the face just as he was coming up.

The German turned to face another Moroccan sneaking up on him. The Arab backpedaled, using his knife to parry the German's attack. That gave his friends enough time to surround the German. Then it was four against one. The man ducked and wove with surprising agility for one so big. The Arabs thrust and feinted, their knives too short to get in close.

A bloodcurdling cry made the Arabs duck and dodge to the side. A Moroccan rushed through the crowd, screaming something at the top of his lungs while gripping his Lebel like a javelin. He wound up and hurled it, his lithe body uncurling like a rubber band. The rifle shot through the air and took the German full in the chest. The Arabs cheered as the man fell to his knees. A moment later they were leaping upon new enemies.

The Germans near the thicket panicked and fled, abandoning their slower comrades to the mercy of the Arabs. The German center, already ravaged by the Vickers, retreated also. That left only the other German flank, which soon withdrew when it saw its support gone.

Within a minute the last German had disappeared into the mist and rain. The Arabs went among the dead and dying, finishing them off and collecting their rifles and ammunition.

"Looks like they finally ran out of bullets for their Lebels," Cole said. Blood trickled from a nick to his right ear.

"Send out a section to help them gather weapons," Thompson ordered. "If the German infantry don't come back, their artillery shells soon will."

"We could be going back and forth like this all week, sir," his sergeant-major said.

Looking at his visibly thinner line, Thompson shook his head.

"We can't afford to, Cole. We can't afford to."

CHAPTER SEVEN

15 September

"Feuer einstellen," Willoughby said.

"Fire installin," Crawford replied.

"Feuer einstellen," Willoughby repeated, slower this time.

"Foyer einstallin," Crawford said, drawing the words out like they were taffy.

Willoughby raised his hands in frustration. "Must you learn this? How about perfecting your use of the King's English?"

"Might come in handy. You shouldn't be the only man in Company E who speaks Hunnish. What if you get blown apart by a shell?"

"Charming thought."

Crawford chuckled. The lad looked more annoyed than worried at that last bit. A fresh-faced university boy putting on upper-class airs with middle-class breeding. How many like him had he seen around Oxford? But Willoughby kept up his end, he'd give him that. Bit weak but he hadn't buckled. Wouldn't neither.

Pity he was such a bloody snob.

Although, on second thought, that was probably what kept Willoughby's chin up. Couldn't stand to look the frightened rabbit in front of the rabble.

As the conversation paused, Willoughby studied him for a moment.

"So tell me more about this copse," the young man said.

"You've been across our side of it going to the darkies, so you know how thick it is."

"And it stays that thick all the way up to the Germans?"

"A few thinner spots here and there but yeah, plenty of cover the whole way until about twenty yards in front of their line. Even there they didn't get some of the bigger trees."

"Mustafa mentioned they'd been sniping at the German working parties."

"Who?"

"The Colonial who came to seek our aid. So you found all this out because you lost your way doing your business?" Willoughby asked with a laugh.

Crawford grinned.

"It was dark and foggy, you remember. And you must say it's a lucky find, sir."

Willoughby bit his lip. Crawford bit his own to keep from smiling. The kid wanted to prove himself. It was a sure bet. And the "sir" would set it in stone. You didn't have to address a mere Corporal as "sir", just "Corporal", but Crawford knew it would clench it. The swot was aching for respect.

Still, Willoughby looked doubtful. "We couldn't keep sufficient men silent for what we'd need up there."

"If we get the jump on them, we won't need numbers."

Willoughby looked off into the distance. "They need a Maxim there for that very reason. It evens out the limited field of fire they're facing. And if we get their Maxim, they'd have to move the one covering this part of the hillside. They're more sure of themselves here than there."

"And who's to say we couldn't manage it a second time?"

Willoughby chuckled.

"I'll go to the Major and request to lead a patrol. I'm the liaison with the Colonials. It would be best to secure our connection with their lines."

Crawford followed as Willoughby clambered down the rough trench, shouldering past men hacking at the hard, wet chalk. He noticed Willoughby walked slowly and with obvious pain. He had an odd gait that looked like he was trying to limp with both legs at the same time. Crawford imagined that if one of the lads bumped into him too hard, Willoughby would collapse like a badly stacked woodpile. The boy had fallen out more than once on the march. Crawford was surprised he'd made it all this way.

They found Thompson and Cole speaking with a messenger from Division. Once the messenger hopped back on his bicycle and sped down the hillside, weaving through the trees with effortless turns, they approached Thompson.

The two young men came up and saluted. Willoughby gave a snappy textbook salute. Crawford's was just on the safe side of sloppy.

"Corporal Willoughby reporting, sir!"

Thompson looked at the young man with an air of friendly familiarity.

"Ah, Willoughby. All's well with the Mohammedans?"

"I've been in regular contact and we've built up a rapport, sir."

"Better you than I. Well, out with it man."

"Private Crawford spotted a weak point in the German line, sir."

Thompson turned to Crawford and gave him a tight smile. "Did he now?"

Crawford stood up straighter. Thompson had given him five days fatigue the previous month for running a dice game. Well, fair's fair, any other officer would have had him behind bars, the army didn't like games of chance, but Thompson hadn't been what you would call delighted.

Willoughby went on.

"He took a wrong turn in the thicket that separates our far right with the French far left, and discovered that it reaches to within twenty yards of the German line."

"He took a wrong turn and walked uphill instead of down?" Thompson frowned at Crawford.

Crawford put on an innocent face. "It was a dark night, sir."

Thompson's frown deepened. Cole's face turned beet red. Willoughby hurried to continue before either of them blew their stacks.

"I would like to send a patrol up there, sir, to see if they have reinforced the position."

Thompson kept frowning at Crawford. "Were you the idiot that woke up the Germans yesterday morning?"

"Couldn't help it, sir. They got the jump on me, sir."

Thompson looked at the crude patch on Crawford's uniform and the dried bloodstain around it.

"You were injured?"

"A scratch, sir. An orderly patched me up. I'm fit for duty, sir."

Thompson grunted to express what he thought of that last statement, then turned to Willoughby. His features softened.

"So you want to take a patrol up there tonight, eh?"

Crawford glanced between the two men. The Major looked indulgent, the young Corporal anxious and eager to please.

He'd guessed right. These two knew each other. All their kind did. Thompson wanted Willoughby to prove himself so he'd have an excuse to recommend him for a promotion, and Willoughby wanted the exact same thing. What Crawford couldn't figure out was why this Oxford student wasn't already an officer. He should be a Subaltern at least.

"While your sergeant should lead the patrol, I'll let you have your chance since you're eager. Don't get too close to the lines, mind you."

"We won't, sir. This is merely to determine the location of their Maxim and strengthen our links with the Moroccans, sir."

Crawford stared at Willoughby with renewed appreciation. The little tosser wasn't a bad liar.

They saluted and left. As they walked down the trench Willoughby said, "The rations are late. Go down and check what's going on. Tell them I said to bring up some extra tea. The men will need it for tonight. And here's some post to give to the quartermaster."

Willoughby handed three letters to him. Crawford put them in his pocket, amazed at what this smooth-chinned corporal felt he could get away with. Just what was the connection between the Major and this lad?

"Yes, Corporal. Nicely done, by the way, Corporal," Crawford said.

"Seems my name is good for something."

"Your name, Corporal?"

"I'm named after my ancestor, as I'm sure you realize. *The* Hugh Willoughby."

"There's more than one?" Crawford asked. *Lord preserve us!*

"Why, the polar explorer, of course!"

"Er, wot?"

"Sir Hugh Willoughby died trying to navigate the Northeast Passage in 1554. He wanted to open a sailing route from Europe to the Orient."

"Why didn't he go through the Suez Canal?"

Willoughby rolled his eyes.

"Because it didn't exist."

"Well he should have dug it then. Would have lived longer."

"Go get the rations!"

Crawford grinned. "Yes, Corporal."

"And no lingering!"

"Wouldn't dream of it, Corporal!"

Crawford hurried down the slope. The Germans had started shelling the Paddies again, and he knew it wouldn't be long until it was their turn. Best to get down and back quick, or better yet get down, wait for the bombardment to start, and stay down until it was over.

I'll blast a Hun to Hell if I have a need to, but there's no way to fight against an artillery shell. I'm not going to get torn apart like poor old Lennox.

Lennox had been a good sort. Always up for a drink or a turn of the cards. A shell got him at Le Cateau. Tore the top half right off him. Nothing left of the poor bugger except his legs and belly.

I'm not clocking out like that.

Crawford passed through the woods and came to a narrow dirt lane cutting through some open fields and past a few scattered farmhouses, now mostly destroyed.

Crawford cocked an ear. The artillery was still hitting to the Connaught Rangers' position. He had a few minutes in the clear at least.

The rain came down at a steady drizzle. Keeping under the shelter of one of the last trees, Crawford took Willoughby's letters out of his pocket and examined them.

"Sealed, the suspicious bugger," Crawford said to himself. He studied the addresses. All relations.

"No girl to write to? I should give you one of mine to make a man out of you. Not that I write them neither. What would I say, 'Dear Elsie, Having a fine time getting shot at. What shirker are you shagging on Saturday nights while I risk life and limb for King and Country?'"

The bombardment of the Irish section of the line began to taper off. Crawford stuffed the letters back in his pocket and hurried on his way. He'd been through enough shelling these past two days to know that once the firing stopped, it would take less than five minutes for the batteries to sort themselves out before they started hitting a new position, and he had a feeling he knew what position that would be.

He jogged down the lane, making good time through an area strangely devoid of people. Everyone was either up on the line or staying well back from it, not that it made much of a difference with the Huns having marked out every blade of grass and cow dropping. The village would be just as hot as the forward trench if the Hun had the mind to make it so.

The only men he passed was a pair of Irish hauling a box of Vickers ammunition between them.

"Seen the breakfast?" he asked as he passed them.

"Not a sodding bite!"

"Me neither, mate," Crawford said, hurrying on.

The German guns were silent as he got to the valley bottom. The lane became wider here and the buildings more numerous. From the moans coming from one it sounded like it had been turned into a dressing station. Another house had been flattened and Crawford spotted the tattered remains of a khaki uniform amid the rubble. Right next to it was a barn with the door open. The muzzle of a field gun poked through.

"Be nice if you lads did a bit of firing!" Crawford called out as he passed. He didn't get a reply.

He was approaching the village now. He slowed down, waiting to see where the German guns would hit next.

It wasn't long before he got his answer. A steady *thud thud thud* sounded from up the hill right behind him. The Oxs and Bucks were getting it.

"Good timing," Crawford congratulated himself. "Your best bet for getting through this with your bollocks still attached is to get promoted to postman."

He strolled into town just as it came to life. Men issued out of buildings, hitching up teams or hauling supplies as officers barked orders. It looked like everyone had been hiding in the cellars for the same reason he had lingered at the edge of town. Now that they knew it was all clear, everyone got back to work.

His nose led him to the field kitchen. He found the head cook, a sour-faced old veteran with a handlebar moustache and a red, sweaty face who was tearing into some nervous recruit as he stirred a giant pot of beans.

Crawford saluted. What an army when you have to salute a cook!

"Urgent request from Major Thompson of the 2/4 Oxfordshire and Buckinghamshire," said Crawford, who saw no reason not to promote and rename Willoughby for the sake of a prompt breakfast. "The men are at the point of exhaustion and will be going on the offensive within the hour. Breakfast urgently requested, sir!"

The cook glowered at him. "Tell the Major he'll get his breakfast when I teach this useless lot the difference between a bean and the boil on a whore's bum."

"I will convey your words to the Major, sir."

"Don't get smart. Tell him the tea will be up in a quarter hour. Breakfast when we're able. Shove off."

Crawford saluted and shoved off. A bit of hunting turned up the quartermaster, who was overseeing the unloading of several ammunition wagons. A work crew was hauling crates into an exposed building. Crawford handed him the letters and put as much distance between him and the explosives as possible.

Wandering down the main street, Crawford looked around. Now what to do? The line was still getting hit, so returning was out of the question, but judging from the state of many of the buildings this wasn't a safe place to muck about in either. Perhaps some of those empty farms he had passed would be worth a look.

Crawford had a habit of looking in other people's houses. The advantage here was there was little risk of anyone being at home. Getting spotted by one irate homeowner in Blackbird Leys had gotten him brought up before the magistrate. If it hadn't been for his brother pulling some strings for him to not only avoid getting kicked out of the Reserves but be placed on active duty, he'd be in jail right now.

"Thanks, Robert," he chuckled under his breath. "Even bet whether you did me a favor or not."

He left town at a fast walk and skipped the first few farms he came to. They stood too close to the village and it was a sure bet that some bastard had already scoured them clean. Further up there might be better pickings.

He spotted a likely prospect. The door was open, creaking in the morning breeze. A large pile of firewood was stacked against the outside wall, covered by a crude clapboard shelter. That was a good sign. If no one had nicked the wood there might be something even better inside.

Crawford entered. The interior was one large room, with a loft above for the beds. A table and a few chairs were scattered about, and a wooden cradle in the corner. The floorboards creaked as Crawford did the rounds. He found nothing but some crockery and an empty tin of tobacco. The family had obviously left taking anything of worth, even the kitchenware.

"Cheap bloody Frogs," Crawford grumbled. "We come to save your country and this is your hospitality?"

He was about to head up to the loft when the whine of an artillery shell made him dive for the floor.

It exploded just outside, making the crockery clink on the mantelpiece.

Crawford scuttled out of the house and across the front yard. A close shave at Mons had taught him that it was best to stay away from any buildings during a bombardment. He didn't want to end up a shredded bit of uniform like that poor bastard in the other farmhouse.

Two seconds later he was proven correct when a second shell made a direct hit on the house. The force threw him flat on the ground.

As the dust settled, Crawford picked himself up. There was a smoking hole where the roof had been. The central beam had crushed the cradle and staved the table in two. A wicker chair just next to it stood undamaged.

Crawford was about to run off when he noticed the beam had accomplished something else. Part of it had crashed through the floor, revealing a cellar underneath. Crawford gave the ridge a nervous look and hurried over.

Yes, a low little cellar. Why hadn't he seen an entrance?

He glanced at the wood pile.

Because they hid it.

Now it was worth the risk to stay a minute or two. Crawford clambered over the debris and lowered himself into the cellar. Lighting a match to see better, he spotted a pile of tools, including several picks and shovels, some bags of flour that had probably been too heavy for them to cart off and (wonder of wonders!) a wine barrel.

Suddenly Crawford didn't mind the bombardment so much.

Later that morning, after the men of the Oxs and Bucks had finally received their breakfast, they spotted a strange apparition coming from the rear. It looked like a metal spider, with sharp limbs sticking out every which way, and the legs of a man wearing khaki trousers below.

Those legs were none too steady. They staggered as much to the left and right as they did forward. As the apparition materialized out of the lingering mist they got a closer look at it. It was a man—they could still not see whom—struggling under the weight of a dozen pickaxes and shovels.

It was staggering from more than that. The mysterious figure was preceded by a waft of cheap wine that could have knocked out anything less than a hardened Tommy. Willoughby gave thanks that Thompson wasn't around. Or Mustafa. What would the Mohammedans think?

With one final stagger the man half-jumped, half-fell into the trench, sending up a tremendous clatter of metal and several choice words from Crawford, who now appeared from beneath his burden, all bleary eyes and unkempt uniform.

"Got some tools, Hugh me laddie," Crawford said in a bad imitation of a Scottish accent. "Let's go shag some sh—"

"Bloody fool!" Willoughby grabbed him by his collar and hauled him down the trench. Crawford stumbled along, tried to keep his footing, failed, and ended up getting dragged by main force down the trench.

Willoughby stopped in front of a group of leering privates.

"You, you, and you, get down the trench, pick up the tools, and start improving the works. Take up enough space that Cole can't pass for a moment. I think I saw him approaching."

"Righto," the laughing crew said, taking off with a mocking salute. Crawford grinned.

Willoughby hauled him to a small dugout he'd made and tossed Crawford inside.

"Ouch! Is that the way you treat you pal?"

"Oh do shut up!" Willoughby shoved him down on the ground and threw a blanket over him. "Pretend you're sick. Stay here and don't make a fuss."

"Aw, and here I was beginning to think you liked me."

"Do you want to be murdered by a member of the English middle class?"

Crawford's face turned into a parody of horror. "Better a Hun or a Lord, sir."

"Then shut the fuck up."

Willoughby hurried down the trench. Just before Crawford drifted off to sleep, he muttered to himself, "He said *fuck*. The swot actually said *fuck*. The things the army does to a man!"

CHAPTER EIGHT

16 September

Just past midnight, Corporal Hugh Willoughby crept through the thicket, barely moving a yard a minute for fear of alerting the Germans not far ahead. He tried to time his steps with the gunfire that crackled from the direction of the Moroccan line. Mustafa had gotten his friends to set up a sporadic fire on their right, far enough down their line to not spook the Germans at this spot, but close enough to distract the ear somewhat.

That had better work, for he had little faith in the *Pickelhaube* and field gray overcoat he wore. Crawford had scrounged them from this very wood. They were damp inside and out and he felt humiliated wearing them. He didn't dare do this in khaki, however.

The Germans would be on their toes thanks to Crawford's shootout. That blaze of fire he had heard the previous night reminded him of Uncle Edward's stories of fighting the Dervishes in the Sudan. They had fired like that, pouring bullets into the air as quickly as they could and hoping for the best. Fearless heathens, though, and damned hard. Uncle Edward had always spoken of them with respect bordering on disbelief.

Up ahead he could see the forest thinning, the black trees silhouetted against dull gray. The light patter of rain masked noise somewhat. He had moved slowly not just out of fear but because his feet still pained him. The charges had been torture. Thank heavens he got to stay prone for much of the time on the line.

On his frequent stops, he perked his ears for the sounds of the five men behind him. They were all from his section, those who were least tired and most eager. Crawford had picked them. The damned cheek.

Still, Crawford was better at this than he. Training on the parade ground at university had been easy enough. All he had had to deal with then was getting shouted at for forgetting some piece of kit or other. Real war, however, had been exhausting and terrifying. He'd been barely able to carry on, and his straggling and physical unfitness had been obvious to everyone.

He envied Crawford's confidence. No one liked him much, but there was no snickering behind his back. He was the company's best shot by a wide margin and one of the toughest as well. Crawford had all the elements of a good soldier but the attitude, while Willoughby had to admit that he himself had the proper attitude and nothing else. He'd joined the University Reserves to please his uncle, never thinking that war would break out in Europe.

To his horror he heard the snap of a twig not far behind him.

The forest fell silent. Would the others be so close? The plan had been to give him enough time to get to the edge of the forest before the rest came up. That way if they were heard he could shout to the enemy in German.

Hardly sporting, but he'd seen good men fall for that white flag trick.

He stood stock still, barely breathing the damp air heavy with woodland musk. Could they see him in here? Doubtful. The Germans were alert, though. He could feel it. He imagined broad Teutonic faces peering into the gloom with alert blue eyes. Mausers with cruel serrated bayonets pointed in his direction. The Maxim gunner with his hand on the trigger guard, listening.

Willoughby forced himself to start counting, forced himself to do it slowly. He would count to ten, no fifty. The others must have stopped at that sound. He'd have time, he hoped. It would be just the thing to have the whole crowd come tramping up before he could get into position.

At the count of fifty he took another step forward, gritting his teeth as a leaf rustled with appalling clamor. Another step, and a third, and the air around him became noticeably lighter. He eased to his left to take advantage of a broad tree. Once behind it, he braced his arm against it and leveled his Lee-Enfield.

Willoughby had timed it perfectly. He sensed more than heard movement behind him. His breath quickened. It would all happen soon now. He'd been exchanging fire with the Germans for two weeks, but his nerves always rattled at the thought. Had Uncle Edward been like this facing those natives charging with muskets belching smoke and swords waving in the air?

Time to find the Maxim. Crawford had said it would be straight ahead, but Willoughby couldn't be sure he hadn't veered in one direction or the other in his creeping voyage up here. The walk wasn't more than five hundred yards but it felt like five miles.

Peering into the gloom, deeper than that of the night before, it took him some time before he espied vague dark shapes silhouetted against a white band. The back wall of the chalk trench had almost a faint glimmer to it, glistening with the rain. Averting his eyes to see better in the dark, he could make out each man as a low black hump. Some wore their helmets, and others did not, assuming they were men at all.

He spotted a larger, squarish hump to his left. The side of the hump shifted, and for a moment he saw the silhouette of a round-shouldered figure wearing a *Pickelhaube*. The man moved and was swallowed by the gloom.

Was that the Maxim? Would it look like that? But of course, there were two gunners, and Crawford had said they'd protected it with logs. Seeing it so far from the side, it looked like a solid mass.

But if he were seeing it at that angle, he was too far away. They'd have to shift left in the face of the enemy.

A breath not far from his ear. Willoughby tensed, almost spun and fired. At the last moment he controlled himself and slowly moved his head.

He saw the outline of a service cap. Crawford, surely. He reached out a hand, touched his shoulder, then turned to look back at the Maxim.

Crawford pressed down on Willoughby's shoulder. *Stay here,* he seemed to say.

Very well, I don't feel like going calling, Willoughby thought. *But know your place and don't give me orders, not even unspoken ones.*

Crawford disappeared downhill. A minute later Willoughby thought he caught a faint whispering. Another minute and Crawford was back.

A tug on the arm to the left. Yes, he understood.

Willoughby crept to the side, closing the distance to the Maxim. Crawford shadowed him from a little further inside the woods.

They made it halfway there when Willoughby kicked something that clunked against the soft trunk of a rain-soaked tree.

From the German trench, a quick whisper and a shuffle as of a few men moving suddenly.

Willoughby and Crawford froze.

"Feuer einstellen," Willoughby said in a soft but clear voice. *"Eine patrouillierender."*

Willoughby swallowed, licked his lips, and stepped out from between the trees. He continued moving toward the Maxim, but angled out from the tree line to be better seen by the Germans.

"Eine patrouillierender," he repeated.

Father had invested a considerable sum in his tutoring. Willoughby hoped the money would be worth it.

One of the men in the trench whispered something Willoughby didn't quite catch. Something about "identification." Willoughby nodded with an exaggerated gesture to make sure they saw him in the dark and continued walking. He spotted a few more shadows along the trench perk up and take on an air of watchfulness.

Willoughby eased his finger away from the trigger guard and curled it around the trigger. He started turning to face the trench.

"*Halt!*"

The clipped order was in the accents of a German, but more than that it was unmistakably that of an officer. No other type of man could get away with such a tone.

Some things the nations of the Earth have in common, Willoughby thought as he aimed at the voice and fired.

An instant later the entire raiding party opened up at ten rounds rapid. The shadows in the trench jerked and dipped down, replaced a moment later by scattered muzzle flares. Over the sound of his own firing, Willoughby heard someone near him fall.

He emptied his magazine, got to one knee and fed in a five-round clip.

A rush around him as the most eager of the raiding party charged forward. Groaning with frustration, Willoughby leapt up with only five rounds in his magazine.

Here's five more than they have, the fools!

A mad run across the narrow strip of cleared ground, a few shots buzzing close, and then onto the lip of the trench. A movement to his right, a silhouette of hand and pistol, and Willoughby pumped two shots into the darkness behind it as he leapt into the trench.

Something soft and heavy tripped him up. Willoughby slammed into the far wall. He managed to gain his footing just as the others all turned to hurry down the trench in the direction of the Maxim.

Willoughby found himself in the middle of the line.

"*Feuer einstellen! Eine patrouillierender,*" He called over the heads of those in front of him.

An excited babble up ahead, cut short by a burst of fire. Willoughby pressed another clip into his magazine and heard a couple of the other men do the same.

A whisper passed down the line from man to man.

"We got her. Leg it."

The men scrambled out of the trench. Willoughby tried to pull himself up, but his exhausted legs didn't have the strength and he slipped back down. A helping hand reached down. He grabbed it and the man hauled him out.

Firing came at them from both directions along the trench, but it was at long range and badly angled, and a quick low run got them deep into the woods. One man slammed headfirst into a tree in a move that Charlie Chaplin would have envied. Willoughby thanked the Lord it hadn't been him.

Bullets snickered through the leaves. A man near him cried out but did not fall. Willoughby got behind a tree, turned, and blindly emptied his magazine. The German shots paused for a moment and everyone hurried on.

He spotted a panting shadow to his right that looked ready to fall down.

"Are you hit?" Willoughby whispered.

Crawford's voice came back to him.

"Bloody heavy, this thing."

Willoughby reached down and felt the Maxim. He grabbed hold. A moment later another man came up.

"Give us a hand," Crawford said.

"All right."

Willoughby recognized Peter Saunders's voice. Their load was suddenly lightened as the big man hefted it. Together they hauled it through the woods.

"Wait." Willoughby stopped.

"The Hun might be after us," Crawford said.

Willoughby tossed aside the *Pickelhaube* and took the overcoat off.

"Wouldn't want to get shot by our own side. Hello, what's this?"

Willoughby felt a flaky crust of dried fluid on the collar. Automatically his hand shot to his neck, only to find it whole. Crawford laughed.

"Sorry I didn't have time to launder it, Corporal."

Willoughby frowned at him, then broke into a smile.

"You gave me a bloodied greatcoat? Crawford, when I make captain, you will most certainly not be my batman."

"There's the pity," Crawford replied.

"Let's go," Willoughby ordered, hearing a new confidence in his voice. They hoisted the Maxim and continued down the slope. The others were all around them, not trying to hide the sound of their movements.

The crack of a Lee-Enfield up ahead made them duck.

"It's us!" Willoughby called.

The noise caused a flurry of firing from the German line, but they were well away and most of the bullets smacked into trees before they ever got near them.

Another Lee-Enfield fired.

"Damn it, it's us you bloody sods!" Crawford shouted.

"Oh, sorry mate."

Sweating and panting, they made it to the firing line and got into the shallow groove they'd hacked from the earth that day. It was barely half the depth of the German trench. Willoughby hoped their little adventure wouldn't set the Germans to shelling again. Saunders pushed the Maxim into the trench with a heavy clunk.

"Pity we didn't get any of the magazines," Willoughby said. "It would have been nice to give them a dose of their own medicine."

"Hey lads, we get any magazines?" Crawford called over his shoulder.

"No."

"Didn't think to."

"Sorry, but—"

"You useless lot, I told you to grab them!"

"Too busy killing Huns," one of them said. Everyone laughed.

"All right, all right," Crawford chuckled.

"We all present?" Willoughby asked.

"Barton got it," someone said. Willoughby remembered the man falling near him when the Germans first opened fire.

"Didn't someone retrieve his body?" he asked.

"I was too busy retrieving my own body, didn't like to leave the poor bugger but—"

"What's all this?" Cole demanded, storming into their part of the trench. Willoughby saluted.

"We were out on the patrol, sir. In the darkness we got a bit too close to their line and they fired upon us. We rushed them, killed at least six, and captured their Maxim, sir."

Cole paused, cocked his head, studying the young man before looking down at the machine gun at his feet.

"I see. Did you sustain losses?"

"Private Philip Barton killed, sir. I was just checking on other injuries."

A quick headcount found two men slightly injured.

"Not a bad exchange," Cole said. "But there's been a bit too much straying around in the woods. It gets them excited and we're liable to be shelled like last time."

A brilliant idea flashed through Willoughby's mind. "With respect, sir, now that we've taken their Maxim we could launch a night assault on that portion of the line, sir."

"With no planning, no proper support, and trying to get a hundred or two hundred men through those woods in the pitch darkness?"

"Well, all we have to do is go uphill, sir."

"With six men you can do that. With two hundred you'll have a mess like we had on the road at Mons. The fellows would be tripping over one another."

Willoughby felt himself blush, and was glad that the darkness hid it. He should have known that. How could he make it to the officer class when someone like Cole could lecture him and be in the right?

Cole turned and went away, probably to make a report to Thompson. Willoughby sat down and let the air out of his lungs in a rush. His heart was pounding. He felt lightheaded and giddy. That had been some little adventure.

Crawford sat down beside him, his wide grin visible in the feeble predawn light.

"I think that went well, considering."

Willoughby felt a flush of pride. After this, surely the men would accept him! He'd earn his way up the chain of command, not be handed a commission like the boys at university.

"Pity about Barton," Willoughby said, suddenly feeling grim.

Crawford looked at him full on.

"He saved a dozen lives at least."

Willoughby thought for a moment and nodded. "Yes, I suppose that's the sort of mathematics we're studying now, isn't it?"

CHAPTER NINE

Private Saunders patted the Maxim gun and chuckled. A good group, this. We'll show the Hun a thing or two!

The gun had been set up behind the British trench, in full view of the Hun just to taunt him a little. Corporal Willoughby had taken the firing pin. "Don't want them taking it in a rush and finding they can use it," he'd said. Nice fellow, that Willoughby, and smart as a tack. Spoke Hunnish like a Hun. When he'd heard the lad call out in the thicket it was all he could do not to put a bullet in him.

Saunders chuckled again and got back to work with his pick. Crawford had liberated some picks and shovels from a nearby farm and the digging went much better now. Crawford was a sharp one too, but of a different sort. More than once he'd seen Crawford's name in the police pages getting done for one little thing or other. Only his good service in the army kept him out of Wormwood Scrubs.

You met all sorts in the army, that was for sure. He could make a good film about Crawford too. *The Thief Redeemed.* That's what he'd call it. Or maybe *From Shirker to Soldier.* That was better. He really had a head for these things. After all this was done he should start up a film studio like that chap in Hertfordshire did.

Now then, how would *From Shirker to Soldier* open? Perhaps with Crawford sneaking into a henhouse. . .

Sergeant-Major Cole's voice broke Saunders off from his fantasies.

"Private Saunders."

"Yes, sir!" Saunders snapped to attention, bringing his pick to his side like a rifle.

"Come with me a moment and bring your rifle."

"Yes, sir!"

Saunders spotted Crawford and a few of the other lads giving him a look.

Cole led him a little downhill and got behind a large tree. The Germans weren't shelling at the moment but it paid to be careful.

"So, Private Saunders, you fellows had a bit of a stroll last night."

Saunders put on a meek face. "It was quite a surprise coming on the Huns like that, sir."

"Yes, Willoughby misjudged the distance. That's what you all said, wasn't it?"

"Oh, it weren't his fault, sir. Dark as the inside of a cask in those woods, sir."

"Crawford got lost in those same woods, and ended up in the very same place."

"That he did, sir."

Cole studied him. Saunders felt himself wilt. The Sergeant-Major was a head shorter than Saunders and at least four stone lighter, but Saunders couldn't meet his eye. He didn't like fibbing to any officer, least of all Cole, who was a good man, but he had to look out for his mates.

And himself.

"How did Willoughby hold up?"

Saunders blinked with surprise at the sudden change in the conversation. For a moment he scrambled for an answer before saying, "Oh, fine, sir, just fine."

Cole didn't look satisfied with this answer, so Saunders went on. "He's a brave lad—er—man, sir. Keen shot too, sir."

"I'm worried about his physical state."

"Oh, well, sir. He's a lot better than he was. We all are what with us sitting in this trench all day. Can't say I prefer it to marching, sir, but it is easier on the legs."

Cole nodded. "Well, I hope your legs are in good order because I need you to deliver a message. Go down to Oeuilly to the divisional quartermaster and bring back a dozen ground sheets and a box of shells for the Major's Webley. Here's a written order."

Cole handed the order to him and Saunders tucked it in his pocket with a sense of disbelief. Surely a messenger could have done this. Then it dawned on him that Cole had wanted an excuse to talk with him. He wondered if Cole was satisfied.

"The corporal will make a fine officer one day, sir. The more experienced among the men have taught him a great deal, and he's not too proud to listen, if you know what I mean, sir."

Cole nodded, and for a moment their different ranks meant nothing as one working man faced another.

"You'd follow him?" Cole asked.

Saunders nodded. "He gets on the wrong end of his share of the jokes, sir, but I'd follow him to Berlin if he asked me. The other lads would too."

"Let's get to the top of this hill first. Go on, private."

"Yes, sir!" Saunders turned, then paused. "If I may, sir, is it true that Corporal Willoughby volunteered as a private? I mean, sir, if you don't mind my saying so sir, as a university lad he could be a junior officer, couldn't he?"

Cole nodded slowly. "Yes, he did volunteer as a private. There was a quite a row at the University Reserves about it too. I'm sure all you men are chattering away like magpies trying to figure out what a gentleman is doing among you lot, so you just go set the record straight. Now get along while it's still quiet."

Saunders didn't need any other incentive. The Hun hadn't shelled their position for more than an hour so they were about due. He'd be glad to be down in the village when that happened. Assuming the village wasn't getting shelled as well.

It was. Saunders arrived at the little cluster of stone houses and shops to find it at the center of a hurricane. As the closest village on the north side of the river, it was being used as a divisional base and the Huns knew it. Just as he made it to the edge of the settlement, moving with care as he saw explosion after explosion and the air hazy with black smoke, a shell shrieked right overhead. Saunders dropped to the ground like he'd been poleaxed.

A deafening roar tore his eardrums and he was flung several feet to the side, smacking down hard on the wet ground. He gave himself a quick, nervous pat down and seeing that everything was where it should be, he looked about him. Not ten yards to his right, a crater smoked and stank.

Licking his lips, Saunders got up and hurried into town.

He arrived just in time for another shell to hit, this time smashing into the roof of a house not thirty yards from him. The roof exploded in a shower of tiles and wood splinters. Saunders curled himself into a ball as the debris clattered onto the street all around him.

"Thanks Candice, you must have lit a candle for me at St. George's," Saunders whispered.

Another man wasn't so lucky. He lay on the ground near the house, head covered in blood. As Saunders got up he stared at the fellow, thinking he was dead. Two privates hurried to the scene and lifted him up. The man groaned and slumped between them. They led him off down the road toward the nearest dressing station.

Saunders rushed down the street in search of the quartermaster's building. He found it in a large barn. The stalls had been cleared out and the place was filled with crates and heaps of spare kit. Saunders paused as he saw dozens of crates of ammunition lying out on the floor. If a shell hit this place it would be all over.

Glancing around, he saw no one about, not even a sentry.

"Hello?" he called out.

"You, what are you doing here?" a voice demanded.

He turned and spotted a nervous young private emerge from a cellar next door, clutching his rifle and looking at him with wide eyes.

"I have a requisition," Saunders said, holding up the paper Cole had given him and feeling rather foolish.

"You have to speak with the quartermaster," the private said, before ducking back into the cellar as another shell shrieked into town. Saunders ducked. The shell exploded two streets away.

"Well, where's he?" Saunders called out.

"I'm coming, I'm coming."

An older man wearing sergeant-major's stripes came out of the cellar. He ran to Saunders, grabbed the paper, and gave it a quick glance.

"Follow me, and hurry!" the quartermaster ordered.

"With respect, sir, you should get a work detail to cover up this ammunition," Saunders said.

"You think I don't know that?" the quartermaster snapped. "No one can spare me the men for a work detail. Everyone's digging trenches. I don't even have any tools. There's not a single entrenching tool in the place, and all the farmer's tools have gone up the hill."

A nearby boom shook the barn. The quartermaster winced.

"Here are the groundsheets," he said, piling them into Saunders' arms. "And the Webley rounds are. . .ah! Here." He handed Saunders a box.

The quartermaster scurried out of the barn and down into the cellar just in time to avoid a shell that landed in the street and knocked Saunders off his feet.

Picking himself up, he gathered the supplies.

"No point staying here," he told himself. "Candice can't afford enough candles to keep you safe in this spot!"

He sprinted out of town, the air queerly quiet. Saunders perked his ears for more distant artillery fire and heard none save for some far to the right, perhaps beyond even those Arabs, and certainly not done by the guns that had just slapped about this town.

In fact, all the guns along the British line, as far as he could tell, had gone silent.

"Bloody hell," Saunders cursed, picking up the pace as much as he could through the ankle-sucking mud. "An attack!"

Several other men must have realized the same thing, because out of cellars and out from behind walls, from ditches and from under wagons came a flurry of soldiers, all running back to the line from whatever tasks had brought them here. All of them squishing through the clinging mud to get back to their mates.

The road turned a bit to the left, and Saunders saw that if he cut through a field straight ahead he could save distance and run free of the worst of the mud, so he veered off, leaving the others still hurrying down the road. He caught an Irish curse as they disappeared in the distance.

It was still raining, and Saunders kept having to wipe his eyes with the groundsheets, which made a cumbersome load that forced him to keep his rifle slung across his back. As he got halfway across the field, just passing a haystack, the soaking groundsheets slipped out of his arms and fell in a heap on the furrows.

Damning his luck, Saunders bent down and started collecting them.

A sound made him pause.

He was sure it had been a voice, but there was no one within sight except for a couple of men back on the road.

It must have been them. Must have shouted and the distance and rain made it sound like a whisper up close, Saunders told himself.

He started collecting the rest of the groundsheets when he heard it again.

This time he was sure it had been close. And even stranger, it didn't sound like English.

He stared and listened, and a moment later heard the voice again.

It was coming from the haystack.

Saunders gaped. He eased the groundsheets down and unslung his Lee-Enfield as quietly as he could. Taking a step toward the haystack, he noticed that it looked a bit tattered, like the hay had been tampered with after it had been stacked. He'd slung enough hay to know.

Another few steps and the voice became obvious. Saunders heard short, clipped words in a harsh language. Words kept repeating, but he didn't know what they meant. They seemed familiar, though.

Numbers?

Saunders fixed his bayonet, wincing at the clatter it made as he slid it around the muzzle of his gun. As the voice went on he made a bold step forward and swiped at the hay with his blade.

Part of the haystack fell away with a rustle to reveal a little cyst, in which hid a bullet-headed man wearing *feldgrau* and holding a field telephone. The man cried out in surprise and slapped a hand on the Lugar at his belt. Saunders fired a bullet into his chest.

The force of the shot threw the German back into the hay, the whole top of the stack collapsing on him before sliding off to the side, leaving the spy sprawled across the remaining pile, half covered in strands the color of honey.

Approaching footsteps made Saunders turn. Several soldiers came running over the field. Saunders let out a breath of relief to see they were British.

A captain led them.

"What's going on here!" the officer demanded. When he saw the dead German and the field telephone he stopped short.

Saunders pulled on the wire coming out of the box of the spy's field telephone. A long black wire cut through the haystack. Saunders followed it, pulling it as he went. The wire tore up out of the ground in a straight line for the German guns.

"Bloody. Hell." He muttered.

CHAPTER TEN

18 September

Thompson wished he and Company E were still up on the line instead of on support. They deserved the rest but at least he would be spared all this paperwork. There were brevet promotions to be made to fill the gaps in the officers, requisition forms to be filled out, and letters to be written to soon-to-be grieving families.

That was the worst. The latest casualty returns showed that of the 227 men that had left England a month before, only 199 were still among the living. No, wait, Smythe had died at the dressing station. 198. And with the wounded he had all of, let's see, 134 men fit for duty.

What, that was all? He'd lost nearly half his men?

Thompson leaned back in his chair and closed his eyes. He could hear the German guns thudding in the distance. None hit close. The bigger guns, the fifteen centimeters, could hit the rear village where he and his men were resting for a day, but they were focusing on something else at the moment. Probably hitting the Royal Artillery batteries that had finally made it across the river.

Oh, to the devil with this damned war! More than forty percent losses and from what he'd heard, his company had gotten off lightly. In fact, he was no longer in command of E Company. Instead, he was now in command of A Company. That company had been hit so hard that it was being melded with his own to make a new A Company. Major Lawson of A Company had a year's seniority on him, but had caught a nasty shell splinter in the face and was being shipped to Paris to recover.

That left him in charge. How fortunate.

Some personal mail had come to him as well. Florence had written to talk about the children. Edgeworth was complaining that boys of fourteen should be allowed to enlist, and Lucilla was knitting him a pair of socks. There were the usual complaints about the servants, and an overly long account of her search for a gardener. These minor issues relaxed him and made him forget about the war for a while. One line, however, brought him to something a little more troubling.

"A Mister Willoughby called," Florence wrote, "asking after his son. Apparently the boy is a corporal in your company. Could you write him and reassure him that his son is doing well?"

Thompson rubbed his jaw. Carstairs Willoughby knew perfectly well that his son was all right, thanks to a word Thompson had had with the military postmaster general about getting his and Willoughby's letters priority treatment. It was one of the many favors he'd done for the senior Willoughby. What the man really wanted to communicate was that he was still waiting, with increasing impatience, for the balance of a rather sizeable private loan Thompson had taken out. While Mr. Willoughby wasn't a gentleman, he tried playing the part and hadn't told Florence the real reason for his visit. Simply showing up at his front door had been communication enough.

So. . .here he was fighting German imperialism while Carstairs stayed home and counted interest.

Where could he get the money? Thompson fretted.

There was a knock at the door of his office, which had been someone's living room in happier times. Cole came in.

"I have the roll for the new A Company for you to check, sir."

More paperwork.

"Thank you, Cole. There's tea in the kettle. Help yourself."

"Very kind of you, sir."

As Cole poured himself a cup Thompson studied him.

"Once all this mountain of foolscap is dug through I'm going to have the compensation of making some recommendations for medals. Saunders is an obvious choice."

"Ah yes, sir. Bit of luck with him finding that German. He's become quite the hero with the men, sir."

"It doesn't seem to have affected the Germans' accuracy."

"No, I suspect there are more spotters skulking about."

Cole sat down at the other chair. Thompson smiled. In peacetime he wouldn't have done that without an invitation, and he wouldn't have received one. War seemed to turn everything around.

"The Lancashires caught one in a coal scuttle," Thompson said.

"Did they, sir? Are they sure it wasn't one of Willoughby's Moroccans?"

Thompson and Cole laughed.

"I need to make some promotions," Thompson said, turning serious. "We've lost too many officers and NCOs. I'm putting you in as captain to replace Briggs."

"That's very kind of you, sir."

"Not at all. You've been doing his work since Mons. You might as well have his rank. Perhaps Brentworth could be made sergeant. Willoughby too."

Cole gave him a curious look. Thompson had said just the day before that Willoughby needed more time before any consideration. The lad insisting on starting the war as a private had thrown everyone into a state of confusion. At least it gave Thompson some scraps to throw the boy's father.

Cole was about to speak when they were interrupted by a knock at the door.

"Come in!"

A messenger entered, saluted, and gave Thompson a note. He read it and glanced at Cole.

"Nesbitt wants to see me at Battalion HQ."

Cole blinked. Majors were not generally called to Battalion HQ. Thompson rose.

"While I'm gone think of some likely men for promotion," he said.

Five minutes later, Thompson gripped the back of a motorcycle as the driver revved his engine and sped past a lorry with centimeters to spare. Air went by in a rush. Rain flicked at his eyes, nearly blinding him. Water and mud sprayed out in the wake of the motorcycle.

This thing didn't seem stable. Four wheels made sense, but this contraption made him remember all the spills he'd taken on his bicycle as a boy. Those had been painful enough, and what speed were they going now? Thirty miles an hour?

And yet he found this didn't bother him as much as it would have a month ago, or even two weeks ago. He still recognized it as dangerous, but the shells and bullets had given him a constant background noise of danger for so long that he had become numb to it all.

The driver swerved around one shell hole and took a smaller one with a jump that nearly threw Thompson off his perch.

That would look good. The first time Nesbitt sees you, you have a sprained ankle. Don't make the second time be with a broken neck.

"What is your name, sergeant?" Thompson shouted into his ear to be heard over the whine of the engine and the rattle of a lorry they were just overtaking and cutting off.

"Kempthorne, sir. Harry Kempthorne. I have a brother who is a medical officer in the First Lincolns."

"But you're a civilian volunteer," Thompson said, noting his lack of a regimental badge. Kempthorne's name sounded familiar.

"I signed up to offer my skills, sir."

Memory dawned. "Ah! You go on exhibition. I've heard of you."

He remembered now. Kempthorne was a stunt driver and cross-country motorcycle racer. He'd won a cup last year in some race or other. Thompson couldn't decide if that made him feel better or worse to be on the back of Kempthorne's machine.

The river leapt into view an instant before they were crossing it. Thompson was surprised Kempthorne could see anything in this downpour. Perhaps the madman didn't see anything at all and drove on instinct. Before the presence of the river fully registered in Thompson's mind they were already rattling across the pontoon bridge, a team of Royal Engineers scrambling out of the way to keep from getting run down.

A deep boom sounded out of the gray blankness ahead. A second boom followed, and a third.

"Here's some bad luck," Kempthorne shouted over his shoulder. "The Hun is shelling Pont-Arcy again. Seems they know every inch of this valley, and know where every one of our important posts is in the bargain."

A blast close to their right made Kempthorne swerve off the road. For a heart-stopping moment Thompson thought they were going to flip over. The motorcycle shuddered and lurched over the edge of a fallow field. Kempthorne hauled the handlebars to the right and got back onto the road.

"Oh, blast!" the driver shouted.

"What is it?" Thompson asked.

"Nicked my handlebars, see?"

Thompson saw a tiny scratch on the shiny reflective surface.

"Sergeant, I don't think that endangers—"

"I just had this bike chromium plated before we left London. Cost me five pounds!"

Kempthorne was about to say more when he was cut off by a honking lorry whose lights flared out of the rain. It came right for them. Kempthorne swerved out of the way. The lorry didn't budge an inch.

"Maniac!" Kempthorne shouted, shaking his fist and making the motorcycle wobble. "Why do they let idiots like that on the road?"

"I am certain that I don't know, sergeant."

They pulled into Pont-Arcy just as a shell crumped into a house and collapsed it. Kempthorne sped down the main street, now abandoned thanks to the bombardment. Thompson could see little through the pouring rain. They pulled up in front of a large stone house. A pair of nervous sentries flanked the front door.

"In there, sir. I've orders to await your return."

"How fortunate for me," Thompson said dryly, hopping off the motorcycle onto his good foot.

He made a fair imitation of a purposeful stride past the sentries, who saluted and ducked as another shell burst nearby, and entered the building.

This had obviously been a private home, now abandoned. Through an open door to the right of the front hall he saw a dining room where a dozen officers tucked into roast lamb and claret, willfully oblivious to the bombardment outside. A quick question to a batsman bringing in a tray of potatoes revealed that Nesbitt was at the end of the hall and to the left in the main operations room.

This turned out to be the living room, cleared of most of its contents and equipped with an oak dining table. Briefly Thompson wondered what home that had come from since this house obviously had kept its own in the original room. Then he remembered himself, stood at attention, and saluted the officers gathered around the table studying a large map and a sheaf of communiqués.

Nesbitt turned to him.

"Ah, Thompson. There you are. How's the wound?"

"My sp—" Thompson stopped himself. He had been about to say "sprain" but realized his commander didn't know how he had been wounded. Best to keep it that way. "My leg is much better. I'm walking fairly well. Most kind of you to ask, sir."

"Right," the officer said, leaning back over the map. "How are the French holding up to your right?"

"Keeping their position in tight circumstances, sir. I have established a bilingual liaison from my company to them, sir."

Nesbitt's brow furrowed. "Didn't the French send their man? We got a note about him. Dupres or something like that."

"We never heard from him, sir."

Nesbitt grunted and went back to looking at the map. He motioned for Thompson to join him.

Thompson studied the map. It was the first detailed one he had seen, a local surveyor's map they had scrounged from somewhere and marked up with the German, British, and French positions.

Those positions told him they weren't making much progress. All along the ridge, and at the base of most of the promontories that pushed into the valley, a blue line signifying the Germans wove along. The British had taken a few of the promontories and pushed their way up the main slope, but at no point had they made it to the top. At the far right of the British line, where his men had been fighting until the day before, he saw that for all the blood spilt, they were no further up than anyone else.

"You and your men fit for the attack?"

"Yes, sir, I did want to see—"

"I ask because I am concerned. I must say I'm a bit disappointed in E Company. I've detected a certain lack of vigor in the advance of our far right. Hopefully the 1/West Yorkshires will do better now that they're holding the line."

Thompson blinked. He felt himself turning crimson as the other officers stared at him.

"With respect sir, charging into the mouth of Maxims—"

"Is a terrible business but the only way to take the German positions. Must I remind you that Joffre sent the Frogs into machines guns at the Marne? They removed the bolts from their Lebels and took the positions at the point of the bayonet. That sort of martial spirit, that *élan*, is just the sort of thing command wants to see from us. And by Jove that's what we'll give them."

Thompson stood a little straighter.

"We will take the position tomorrow, sir. But we will do it with fewer losses if we prepare first."

"The artillery is doing the best they can with the terrain given them, better now that the Royal Flying Corps is sighting for them."

"I'm not speaking of the artillery, sir," Thompson said, producing the Maxim's firing bolt from his pocket. "My men took this from the Germans last night. They brought back the whole gun, as a matter of fact. It's making quite the trophy in our trench. Excellent for morale, sir."

The officer blinked and looked at the hunk of Krupp steel. Thompson gave it to him.

"Compliments of the company, sir."

Nesbitt chuckled. "Well done, Thompson, but surely the Germans will simply replace one Maxim with another."

Thompson nodded. "That they will, which is why I want to send raiding parties to our front to take both Maxim guns an hour before the attack is launched."

"Are you mad? It will put them on alert. Might as well announce our intentions with a bullhorn!"

"I don't think so, sir. My men have been harassing the Germans every night since we got here. It keeps them on the back foot and stops them from launching the night raids that the Irish and some others have suffered. Plus it keeps up morale. If we don't raid tonight, they will get more suspicious than if we do, sir."

The officer's brow furrowed. "And who authorized these raids, Major?"

Thompson swallowed. "I did, sir."

Better to tell a lie than admit I can't control what some elements of the company do at night. If we weren't in battle, I'd have Crawford thrown in the battalion guardhouse. But what could I do with Willoughby?

"And what have your results been, other than one machine gun?" Nesbitt asked.

"Fifteen confirmed killed and an unknown number wounded."

"And your losses?"

"One killed and two slightly wounded, sir."

"If accurate, those numbers are quite impressive."

"The men appear to have some talent for it, sir," Thompson said, deciding to ignore his superior's skepticism.

The higher officers exchanged glances. The lieutenant-colonel studied the bolt in his hand. "Two simultaneous raids in the pitch darkness in what almost certainly will be a heavy rain? This could end badly, Major."

"We will lose men, sir, but not as many as we would if we charged those guns at first light tomorrow, sir."

Nesbitt got a distant look to his eyes. "Yes, it's been a bloody business, a terribly bloody business." He suddenly looked Thompson in the eye. "You were in South Africa, were you not?"

Thompson met his gaze. "Yes, sir."

Nesbitt nodded slowly. "So was I. I daresay this will be much worse. Fighting the Boer we had to start thinking in new ways. Cut up the land with barbed wire and blockhouses to slow their movement. Enlist the natives. I suspect we'll have to do some new thinking in this war as well. All right, Thompson, you'll have your way. The Ox and Bucks will move up to the support line, and you can take out your raiding parties and do your best, but we won't delay the attack by a single minute. I hope for the sake of your men they aren't still out there when the show begins. The Yorkshires are keen to get into the fight. You won't want to get in their way."

Thompson ground his teeth. He resented the man's tone but what could he do? All he could do was salute and leave. He fumed all the way out of headquarters and down the street to where Kempthorne awaited him astride his bike, sheltered by the umbrella of a wide-spreading oak. Thompson greeted him cursorily and climbed on back of the machine.

Kempthorne revved the engine, and in a spray of mud spun it around 180 degrees. Thompson lurched backwards as Kempthorne gunned it down the lane, swerving onto the shoulder when a cavalry horse panicked at his approach. Kempthorne righted the machine at the last moment, got into the middle of the road, and shot back toward the support line with the curses of the cavalryman following them in futile pursuit.

I'll show Nesbitt what the Oxs and Bucks can do. But before I can do that, first I have to survive this maniac.

CHAPTER ELEVEN

Captain George MacDonald led a stretcher party into the valley and through a cluster of small homes and shops called Verneuil. It lay just south of the base of one of the many promontories that divided the valley. Fortunately this was one of the few that the BEF had taken and was thus free of direct fire. The RAMC had established 2nd Division's collecting station and surgery at a large, three-story chateau just beyond the last houses.

While MacDonald preferred to stay at the front line, one of the wounded was a bad case and needed his constant attention on the way down. The man's guts had been fricasseed by a shell splinter and there was no saying whether he'd make it or not. Another man had a bad head wound. There had been many of those since the men had dug in.

Perhaps the High Command should start issuing service caps made of metal, MacDonald thought.

Behind the stretcher bearers came three walking wounded, two who had had their faces cut by shell splinters and another fellow who claimed have accidentally shot his finger off while cleaning his rifle. MacDonald wasn't sure what to do about that case beyond putting a tourniquet on the stump and writing a report. He'd leave any hard decisions to Major Thompson.

MacDonald and his stretcher party hurried across the chateau's lawn as a German shell sent up a plume of mud not far down the road. A horse's scream cut the air. He saw several men running from the blast. A quick glance satisfied him there were no human casualties. Like everywhere else in this valley, the German guns had this spot well marked out. They didn't need to directly see the village to shell it.

The chateau was an ornate affair with a Gothic tower and carved columns. So far it had escaped unscathed except for some broken windows. The large Red Cross painted on the gabled roof may or may not have helped. Beyond five broad stone steps the large double doors stood open. The front hall, lined with suits of armor and medieval tapestries, had been turned into a dressing station for new arrivals. A sweeping marble staircase led to an upper story where the staff had installed the surgeons' quarters. Some stretcher bearers bringing a groaning man upstairs made him realize the surgeons were now going to be sharing space with an increasing number of patients.

MacDonald told most of his party to deposit the less serious cases in the front hall and get back to the line. He led the bearers of the shrapnel case and the head wound through an open door below the stairs to the back of the house and the operating room.

This had once been the salon. The furniture had all been removed but an elegant gold-framed mirror still hung above an ornate hearth. Portraits and old landscapes adorned the papered walls. From the ceiling hung a chandelier of burnished gold. Tucked in the corner MacDonald saw a sterling silver liquor tray on wheels, now devoid of its contents.

MacDonald grunted. Back home they would have stolen the tray, not the liquor. It must be worth ten pounds at least, but who had use for such a thing out here?

The room had four operating tables, all occupied. The head surgeon manned the table next to the door. He was just extracting a bullet from a lung as MacDonald came in.

MacDonald reported to the orderly, who took one look at the gut case and put him at the head of the queue. An explosion outside rattled the scalpels in their pans and the liquor set at the far end of the room.

"I need two packs of field dressings and a hundred grams of morphine," MacDonald told the orderly.

"All requests through the chief dispenser," the orderly told him.

"And where can I find—"

A great crash to the front of the chateau cut off MacDonald's question. A shell shrieked right through the door he had just entered, blurred across the operating room, and smashed the mirror over the fireplace.

"Crikey!" MacDonald cried out, leaping in the air.

The surgeon plunked the bullet into a waste pan, sewed up the punctured lung, and stepped back from the patient as the nurse moved in to suture the chest. He examined the shattered mirror and the smoking crater in the wall.

"Broken it, eh? That's bad luck for the Germans!"

"Don't the damn Huns know the meaning of a Red Cross?" grumbled the orderly.

"More than once they've pretended to surrender only to fire at our chaps," MacDonald replied, wiping his brow and looking fearfully at the smoking mirror. He collected himself and turned back to the orderly.

"You were about to tell me where the chief dispenser is?"

"Upstairs," the orderly replied. "Second door on the left."

MacDonald and the four stretcher bearers went up the stairs, their steps silent on the plush red carpet. MacDonald noted it was stained and blotched in places. One of the stretcher bearers, a man named Morris who played the trombone in the regimental band, looked at the stains and chuckled.

"Looks like the Frenchies will have to do some redecorating when all's said and done."

"The Germans are redecorating for them!" said Andrews, another stretcher bearer. "Captain MacDonald, want to lay odds on whether or not this mansion will survive the battle with one stone upon another?"

"Seven to one against," MacDonald grumbled.

"That's generous," Morris said. "I give it ten to one. We're stuck here till Christmas at the earliest."

"That's quite enough, private," MacDonald said, pulling off his service cap and wiping his bald spot. He was still rattled by the near miss in the surgery and the last thing he needed was a bunch of privates spouting grim truths.

Passing a closed door through which the screams of dying men assaulted his ears, MacDonald found the dispensary. It was staffed by a preoccupied-looking chemist who passed MacDonald the items he requested and immediately went back to studying a requisition form.

"Too bloody slow. Everything's too bloody slow. . ." he kept muttering.

MacDonald gave him a backwards glance as he left the building. There was a muffled boom and the floor vibrated beneath his feet.

"Better off back at the line," Morris griped.

"We'll be there soon enough," MacDonald said.

They emerged from the chateau to find Verneuil shrouded in a gritty haze. Plumes of smoke rose from three different buildings that MacDonald could see, and he guessed the Germans had hit several more.

They hesitated at the doorway. For a full minute the shells didn't come.

"Have they stopped?" Morris asked no one in particular.

"Sometimes this means they're shifting, sometimes this means they're having a fag," Andrews muttered.

"Let's chance it. This place is a target," MacDonald said. He hurried down the steps and the four privates closely followed.

They stuck to the side of the road, where trees and buildings might shield them from a blast. On the edge of the village they came upon a supply wagon that had taken a direct hit. The horse team lay in butchered ruin across the width of the road. The driver was in even worse shape, his remains so mingled with those of the horses that with some chunks of meat it was impossible to tell man from beast. Another soldier lay a few feet away, his chest opened and bloody, yet still heaving in painful breaths.

The medical team rushed over to him. A few seconds told MacDonald all he needed to know—even if this man were lying on a surgery table back at the chateau he would be dead in a matter of minutes. MacDonald gave him an injection of morphine.

"Look, another one," Morris said, pointing.

A figure in khaki lay stretched out in the front yard of a cottage. One hand raised and covered the face, then waved slowly back in forth, not to signal to the team, for the face was averted, but as an expression of agony and despair.

MacDonald ran over. The image of a harp on the man's brass cap badge told MacDonald he was from the Connaught Rangers. A leather dispatch bag lay by his side. The wound was on the front inside of the shoulder. His arm looked like it was dislocated and the clavicle shattered. The man's face twisted in stunned agony. His eyes were closed and his other arm kept rising to his face and then falling back to the ground.

The men laid down the stretcher as MacDonald pinched off an artery and stuffed the wound with gauze. Andrews gave the Irishman a shot of morphine while MacDonald kept pressure on the wound. After a minute they lifted him onto the stretcher. The man's breathing and pulse showed no great danger. They trotted down the street, MacDonald still pressing on the wound. No more shells came.

"You're in luck," MacDonald told his patient, "We're just two minutes away from the surgeon. He'll have you on the mend and going home by sunset."

MacDonald meant it, and it felt good to be able to say so.

A sudden detail made him look around at his team.

"Did any of you pick up his satchel?"

The privates glanced at him dumbly, still trotting for the chateau.

"He's a dispatch runner! We can't just leave it there," MacDonald scolded them.

"I'll get it, sir," Morris said.

"No, press down here. Yes, that's right. I'll get it. It should be carried by an officer."

MacDonald turned back and jogged over to the bag. Just as he bent to pick it up there came a high-pitched shriek. The neighboring yard erupted in a plume of dirt. A large oak tree groaned and fell over. It slammed to the ground, the explosion puffing its foliage out in a cloud.

"Sir?" Morris called. The stretcher bearers gaped.

The leaves settled. MacDonald, covered in dirt and leaves, crouched just within the V of the two main branches.

A few inches to either side and he would have been pulped.

"Crikey!" MacDonald gasped.

"You all right, sir?" Morris called again.

"Yes." The word came out as a whoosh of air. MacDonald bent over, almost lost his balance, and tugged at the dispatch bag, which was stuck under one of the branches. One pull. Two. He yanked it out from under the branch, stumbled over the other branch, and started weaving his way back toward his men.

"Twice in one hour!" one of the stretcher bearers said in admiration. "Someone's Ma is praying hard."

"Nearly snuffed it when the Hun raised the white flag," said another. "Saw it myself, I did. Got his cap shot right off his head. Would have parted his hair if he had any."

"Bloke's magnetic."

"Magnetic MacDonald, that a good one!" Morris cracked.

CHAPTER TWELVE

Crawford cursed under his breath as he ground away at the end of an entrenching tool with a file. He sat in a chalk cave, one of many the Frenchies had dug into the hillside to shelter livestock. It was cold, clammy, and stank of goat shit, but at least it protected them from bombardment.

He sat on an upturned bucket with a heap of entrenching tools spread out before him. Other men from his unit sprawled all around, mostly asleep or speaking in low tones. Cigarette smoke hung in the air in a thick haze. He was the only one working. Cole had given him fatigue duty without saying why. Probably for that stunt he had pulled in the copse.

Typical. I perform heroics worthy of a Victoria Cross and they promote me to chief knife sharpener. What's next, digging a latrine?

He only wished he could have nicked more picks and shovels. There weren't enough to go around, so most of the lads were still stuck trying to break chalk with these worthless things.

Saunders' annoyingly upbeat voice broke the quiet.

"Good billet, this. Nice and cozy."

That big oaf started humming some tune.

"How can you be so bloody cheerful in this muck?" Crawford snapped.

"Would you like to be in a film?" Saunders asked with a grin.

"Wot?"

"Oh, nothing."

Crawford grunted and went back to sharpening the entrenching tool.

"I wonder how long they'll keep us in support?" Saunders asked no one in particular.

"Don't question your luck," another private answered.

"Luck," Crawford snorted, filing away at a battered shovel blade.

"Speaking of luck," another man piped up, "have you heard of Magnetic MacDonald?"

"Who?" Saunders asked.

"You know, Captain MacDonald the doctor. He's the luckiest man alive."

"How lucky could he be? He's here, isn't he?" Crawford grumbled.

"Oh, he may be here but he might as well be enjoying the sights at the Crystal Palace. He's invincible. Morris, you know Morris, the trombone player, he's in the stretcher party and says the man is positively magnetic. Morris was up on the line the other day and saw a bullet pluck MacDonald's service cap right off his head. MacDonald bent down, put it back on, and bless me if I'm lying but another bullet took it right back off his head again!"

"Are you joking?" someone asked.

"Got it straight from Morris. And that wasn't the only time. When they were taking wounded down to Verneuil two shells nearly got him. One chased him right across the surgery!"

Crawford stopped his work and stared at the man. "The Huns are hitting the hospital too?"

"They're not civilized, you know that. You've heard what they're doing in Belgium."

Crawford grunted and went back to filing.

"As I was saying, the shell went right past him, blew off his cap again, and smashed a mirror on the wall right next to him."

"Must have turned him into mincemeat, the poor chap," Saunders said.

"There's where you're wrong, he wasn't even touched! Glass flew all around him, cut up a dozen doctors and patients and he just stood there as easy as you please without a scratch on him."

"Sounds like he doesn't have good luck, he's got bad luck but it goes onto everyone else. I've heard about people having that power," one man said, a tremor in his voice.

Crawford gave him a sour look. "Next you're going to say MacDonald's Ma is a cunning woman and wrapped some fingernails in a dried frog's skin and tucked it in his cap."

The man gaped at Crawford. "Is that how they do it?"

Crawford snorted and went back to work.

We'll never win the war with this pack of idiots.

Sergeant-Major Thomas Cole entered the cave. Crawford resisted the urge to spit.

A few of the newer men saluted, but the old hands stayed as they were. Cole didn't hang on regulations when Thompson wasn't around.

"Evening, lads, get your rest while you can because we may be going up in the morning."

"Already, sir?" Saunders asked as Cole sat down.

"The Major has been called to Battalion HQ. That's never a good sign."

"I'd rather be shooting Germans than sharpening shovels," Crawford grumbled.

"You'll obey orders and like them, private," Cole said. The look he gave Crawford wasn't as hard as it would have been coming from another officer. Crawford had to admit that Cole was the least bad officer he'd ever served under. Thompson wasn't half bad either, although he played favorites and was a stickler for some rules.

Cole massaged his knees, wincing as he did so.

"Still sore from the march, sir?" Crawford asked, unable to keep a bit of malicious delight from his tone.

"That I am, that I am," Cole said, pulling off his boots.

"If you don't mind my saying so, sir, you're a bit long in the tooth for this, aren't you sir?"

Cole shrugged. "I suppose I am. Got two girls at home as well."

"Aw, it's a wonderful thing to have a little girl to dandle on your knee!" Saunders said. "My little Anna—"

"You could have gotten out of the call-up," Crawford said to Cole, surprised he hadn't.

"Well, I was convinced otherwise."

"How's that?"

"In civilian life I'm Major Thompson's gardener."

Well that explains how you made Sergeant-Major, Crawford thought. Cole continued.

"When war was declared last month Major Thompson reported for duty, as was right. I was still mulling things over when young Master Edgeworth came to see me."

"Who's that?"

"Major Thompson's son. Fourteen years old and a fine lad. He'd have signed up if he'd been given half the chance."

"He might still get it," one of the privates grumbled.

"None of that, now. So one fine morning I'm trimming the hedges when young Master Edgeworth comes up to me. Gives me a grand speech about patriotism and duty and the rights of small nations. A grand speech. If he had given it at school he would have gotten top marks. I just got on with my work and listened and nodded as you do."

Crawford smirked but said nothing. The toffs always assumed you looked up to them unless you set them straight, and Cole wasn't the kind to do that. Crawford wouldn't mind opening Willoughby's eyes about a thing or two.

"The lad finally says his bit and went off. I didn't think much of it. The next day Major Thompson comes up to me while I was pruning the rose bushes. He was about to head to the barracks to see to their opening and was already wearing his uniform. We talked about the garden a bit and the weather and a few other things here and there. Then he sighs and looks out across the fields all dreamy like."

Probably thinking he'll miss the hounds, Crawford thought.

"'This month certainly is a scorcher,' he says."

"'It most certainly is, sir,' I says."

"'Not as bad as the summers in South Africa,' he says."

"'No, sir, not as bad as that.'"

"'But the nights! How could a land so hot in the day be so cold in the night?'"

"'I'm sure I don't know, sir. As cold as the dead of an English winter.'"

"So he's still looking over those fields, looking out and not seeing what was before him. The good Major goes silent for a moment and I'm thinking he's about to head off, but then he says all quiet, 'And the mountains. Remember how we had to share blankets to keep warm? How we couldn't light a fire to even make some tea for fear of the Boers spotting us?'"

"'They were frightfully good with those Mausers, sir,' I says."

"'That they were,' he says. 'And no matter how many nights we went without fire and how well we hid ourselves, they'd always root us out. Attack when we were laid low with cholera or suffering from heatstroke or exhausted after a march.'"

"'Yes, sir, hard times they were. Hard times.'"

"Then he looks right at me, Major Thompson does. Not toward you like they do, but at me. And he says, 'It looks like we're in for it all over again, Cole.'"

"And I look right back at him and say, 'Yes sir, it looks like we are.'"

CHAPTER THIRTEEN

Thompson peered through a drenching rain into the pitch black night. He heard nothing except for the steady patter of drops on wet grass. He could barely see ten yards. This place unnerved him.

He was in the space between his trench and the Germans', crawling along ground he had run across just a few days before. He had been through this stretch of ground four times before, leading four bloody, futile charges.

Then it had been terrifying, a mad rush through bullets and blood for a line he never reached, but now, now he crawled through black silence toward the muzzles of unseen guns.

And that was far, far worse.

Cole was at his side, and behind came Willoughby and four privates, including that shirker Crawford, who for some reason Willoughby seemed to take stock in.

Thompson paused. Through the gloom he espied a dark form on the grass, a hump that didn't move. He stared at it. A rock?

A hand touched his shoulder. He looked to his right. Willoughby lay next to him. The corporal pointed at the shape and ran his forefinger along his throat.

Thompson looked again. Yes, it did look like a body. Surely there was no shortage of those out here. He crawled forward a few feet and saw Willoughby was right.

From Magdalen College to France and you're still learning, eh my boy? You're a sharp one. Perhaps you really are officer material. Your shopkeeper of a father certainly seems to think so. Perhaps I can get a few month's reprieve from him if I make you sergeant.

They moved forward, leaving the dead man without even looking to see if he was one of their own. They had other things to do.

They passed more bodies, unrecognizable as German or British in the darkness. Thompson looked back at his men and saw Crawford taking up the rear in a zig zag. After a moment of watching him it became apparent that he was going to each body within easy reach and feeling for their helmets. Crawford was counting. Thompson reminded himself to ask Willoughby what the final count was.

After another few yards of quick but careful advance they came to the spot that Thompson wanted to see. A swale in the hillside offered some cover. A dark shape loomed at its far side. Thompson remembered it was a gnarled tree stump, split and chipped by gunfire. It had been a grand old oak from the looks of it, and its stump was broad enough to cover three men lying side by side. It also gave a decent vantage point of the Maxim, not that they could see it in this gloom.

Cole drew up close to him and whispered in his ear. "That other dip in the land is thirty yards to the right and a bit down slope. Let's see that after this."

Thompson nodded and edged away. Cole's breath was hot and smelled of bully beef.

Thompson waved to the line behind them and pointed off to the right, then started that way himself. The men moved out.

A faint whistle made him look over this shoulder and freeze. A pair of shadows flitted away from the larger blot of the stump, heading in a straight line for the German trench.

Damn it, they know we daren't fire.

Everyone rushed at the two Germans as quickly as they could without making much noise, praying the two didn't lose nerve and shout out. The Germans knew if they did that Thompson and the rest would gun them down. The two Huns had traded silence for a race they might win.

Crawford and Willoughby were the first to catch up, with Willoughby running at a flailing painful gait. Cole came just behind. The two Germans turned at the same moment and leveled their guns. Crawford swiped the butt of his rifle across the man's face like the slap of a nine-pound hand of wood and steel. The German's body hit the wet grass with a loud smack.

Thompson's gaze flicked over to catch Willoughby and his opponent facing off, feinting and darting around each other. The German lunged. Cole leapt into the fray and batted the German's weapon up and to the side an instant before he would have planted his serrated bayonet into Willoughby's chest. Willoughby jammed his bayonet into his opponent's belly an instant later.

The man let out a gasp, which was cut short when Willoughby yanked out his weapon and gouged it into the German's throat. Thompson saw the German's silhouette writhe and fall. The man made a sick, choking sound and twitched for a moment before lying still.

Thompson looked back at Crawford. The private gave his opponent another hit on the head with the butt of his rifle. The German didn't move.

For a second there was silence. The men turned to go.

The shadowed column froze again, this time to a faint call in German from up the slope. Silence. Rustling. The call again, more demanding. They could see nothing. Thompson gestured wildly to his men and hurried down the slope for their own lines. They ran with bodies low, tense, waiting for shots to bark over their shoulders. None did. With a whispered password they slipped into their own trenches to find the guards on duty watchful and telling of a silent night.

Later, Thompson and Cole sat sipping lukewarm tea and discussing the possibilities.

"We should see that position," Thompson said. They sat in the trench, listening to all quiet for an hour now.

"I can take you there. Not much to see, sir," Cole said.

Thompson looked at the white chalk of the trench wall as if he could see back to headquarters and catch them watching.

"I daresay there isn't, but if we're to do this raid I'll want to know it."

"Same party?"

"Same party."

Thompson caught a low cursing as Cole ordered the men to prepare.

They hauled themselves over the lip of the trench, more than one man slipping or scrabbling on the wet chalk that stained them all far too bright of a hue, and crawled straight up the slope. Thompson kept looking down at his uniform to check the chalk was wiping away on the wet grass. Yes, he was getting good and dark now.

Cole hadn't misremembered. Just a slight veer to the right and they found it. It was a cut into the slope, like someone had removed a tree stump or an outcropping of rock years ago. It had since weathered into a firm bowl of grass that could cover two men decently or one man well. Being a bit back from the bigger swale they'd already investigated, it didn't have as good a field of fire as the other one, but it was cover nonetheless.

A plan formulated in Thompson's mind. He'd select the five best shots from the company and send three to the left swale and two to this one. Well, with the exception of Crawford, who was the best shot of them all. His services would be needed on Willoughby's raiding party. Once the men were in position, Thompson would lead a raiding party between the two positions and get as close as he could to the German trench. When they were noticed, they would rush in while giving them rapid fire. The men in the two swales would fire straight forward into the machine gun's flanks. This would give them support and avoid anyone getting plugged in the back by an English bullet. After disabling the Maxim, the raiding party would then retreat straight back.

In the meantime, Willoughby would lead a second party up the copse to take out the Maxim gun in position there. The boy had told him a Moroccan scout had spotted the Germans replacing the one they'd stolen. A pity, but not unexpected.

As Thompson led his men back down to the line, he turned over the possibilities in his mind and felt a twinge of doubt. Dare he let Willoughby lead the second party? He was only a corporal so it would be highly irregular, but Saunders and Crawford would be with him. Saunders had a good head on his shoulders, and Crawford, while a cad, was an excellent man in an emergency.

Besides, Willoughby had managed success once before. It was only fair to let him try again. If all went well, he'd be justified in recommending Willoughby for a promotion and Florence would receive no more visits from Willoughby's father.

Thompson didn't want to think about what that blasted moneylender would do if Willoughby was killed.

Soon enough I'll be charging into a Maxim. I may not have to worry about my debts for long.

The raid needed a diversion, though. Nothing too big, no artillery. That would surely get the Germans' wind up. No, perhaps some skirmishing to either flank. Willoughby had been a clever lad to have the Colonials keep up a fire during that scouting party. That had muffled their sound and given the Germans something else to pay attention to. Would they fall for the same trick twice? He supposed he was already expecting them to by trying to take that position a second time. Very well, he'd have Willoughby talk with the Colonials. He wouldn't ask the Irish, however. They were too hotheaded. They would most likely start a full-on offensive and muck up the whole show. He'd just warn them to stand to. Once the firing started—and he had no doubt there would be a great deal of firing—the Irish could do whatever they liked, as long as it was noisy.

The scouting party slipped back to the English lines. Thompson led them back to the support position and ordered them to get as much sleep as they could. They'd need it.

CHAPTER FOURTEEN

Willoughby led his raiding party along the rough trench that cut through the copse between the British and Moroccan lines. He needed to speak with Mustafa about starting a diversion for tonight's adventure, and he had decided to bring along the men so they could meet the Colonials.

It was best that the men know who was supporting them. Thankfully Crawford's breath contained not a whiff of alcohol. The Mohammedans might not approve.

He liked these African chaps. They didn't judge him by his accent or subtly press him for information about where he went to school. Of course they wouldn't know the significance of the answer. Their ignorance was his bliss.

They picked their way through the woods, finding it easier to walk slightly behind the narrow trench than trying to squeeze past the men of the 1/West Yorkshires positioned there. They were defending most of the copse as well. At its eastern end, where the trees thinned out, the khaki of the British troops gave way to the red fezzes, blue vests, and white pantaloons of the Colonial troops.

Mustafa was there to greet them.

"Bonjour, mon ami," the sergeant said, a grin brightening his dark face.

"Hello again. Thank you for your help with the last raid," Willoughby replied in French. He still couldn't get over the fact in the past week he'd had more opportunity to practice his French with an Arab than with any French people.

"And thank you for getting medicine and weapons to my comrades and I. Because of this, some men who would have died will now live to see their homes again. For this I want to give you something."

Mustafa pulled a curved knife out of his belt and presented it to Willoughby.

The corporal took it and turned it over in his hands. The scabbard was made of worked brass with elaborate arabesque etching. The handle was of smooth dark wood with a guard and pommel of etched brass. The lines of the etchings wove in and out of each other, making complex, repeating patterns.

"It's a *koummya,*" Mustafa explained. "The traditional knife of my country. Check the blade."

Willoughby drew it and studied the curved, ten-inch blade. Crawford gave an appreciative whistle. Willoughby tested its edge with his nail. Razor sharp.

"This is Arabic, yes?" Thompson said, pointing to some squiggles carved on the blade near the hilt.

"It says 'God is Great.'" Mustafa said. "Turn it over."

There was more Arabic writing on the other side, in clean, crude lines that showed it had been recently made by a less-than-expert hand.

"That says 'Willoughby.'"

Willoughby gave a sheepish grin. "So that's what my name looks like in Arabic."

Growing serious, Willoughby put a hand on Mustafa's shoulder. "I'll treasure this."

"It is not meant to be treasured, my friend, it is meant to be used."

Willoughby glanced up at the ridge.

"I suspect I'll be getting a great deal of use out of it."

"Is he giving that to you?" Crawford asked. The rest of the raiding party had been standing around, looking frustrated that they couldn't follow the conversation.

"Yes he is," Willoughby said with pride.

"It was owned by Abdullah Idrissi," Mustafa said. "One of the men. He died and he did not have a son, so we are free to give it to another man."

"Abdullah Idrissi," Willoughby repeated, nodding. "I'll remember that name."

"Come, let's have tea," Mustafa said, leading them down the line.

"Where are we going, Corporal?" Saunders asked.

"For tea, private," Willoughby said.

Saunders brightened and nodded at Mustafa. *"Merci!"*

Mustafa smiled back and shook his hand. This led to a round of hand shaking and introductions. Then the soldier led them to a small fire.

"So you're getting supplies again," Willoughby said to Mustafa.

"Bullets yes. Still no doctors except for your team. Some food, but this tea we make ourselves."

A few other men sat in a circle in the hollow left behind by some old diggings. A low fire burned there, protected from the rain by a ground sheet stretched on corner strings fastened to four trees. The damp wood smoked badly, but all the men were smoking cigarettes anyway and seemed not to notice.

The Arabs beckoned them to sit. Willoughby looked around the circle and noted a wide range of features. Many looked Arab like Mustafa, while one was so light as to be almost white, and several more were Negroes. He hadn't realized there were so many races in Morocco.

One of the men took a pot off the fire and filled several tin cups with a piping hot red liquid.

"Tea from Morocco," one of the Negroes said in passable French. "Sorry we have no sugar."

"Thank you," Willoughby took the first cup. As the others were given some he translated, "No sugar, lads," his voice cracking at the forced familiarity of "lads".

"Ah, sugar! Remember sugar?" Saunders chuckled.

"I remember I haven't had it for nearly two weeks!" Crawford grumbled.

Willoughby took a sip of his tea. "Interesting flavor."

"You like it?" the Moroccan asked.

"It's very nice."

"It's better with sugar."

"It's better with no one shooting at us."

Mustafa laughed.

Saunders pulled out a packet of cigarettes.

"Smoke?" he asked around. Crawford reached for it and Saunders slapped his hand away.

"Get your own, you blighter. These are for the darkies."

Crawford pretended to look hurt. "You'll give unbelievers a smoke before a good Christian?"

"The only thing Christian about you is the country that spawned you," Saunders ribbed him.

The Moroccans each took a cigarette. Saunders pointed to one of the smokes and said in exaggerated slowness.

"Cig-a-rette."

One of the men nodded. *"Oui, cigarette."*

"Oi, he's a fast learner!"

"The word is the same in French, Private Saunders. In fact it's where we got the word," Willoughby informed him.

Saunders chuckled. "Fancy that. I've been speaking French the whole time!"

Willoughby looked down at his new knife, turning it over to examine the intricate decoration.

"So tell me about Abdullah Idrissi," he said to Mustafa.

"He was a good man. Older than you, though not so old. No wife. He was a true patriot."

Willoughby studied him.

"When you say that, you mean a patriot of Morocco."

"Of course! I too am a Moroccan patriot."

"But you fight for France."

Mustafa made a face.

"I do not like French people. They are arrogant, not like the English."

Willoughby fought a smile. Mustafa went on.

"Some day we will kick all the French out of the country and be ruled by a Muslim again."

Willoughby cocked his head.

"You don't like the French yet you fight for them?"

Mustafa grinned and shrugged. "My country is poor, Willoughby, and the French pay well. And the Germans want Morocco too. If they defeat France they will invade my home. The French give us guns and money to fight the Germans, so we fight them."

"Better the devil you know than the devil you don't," Willoughby said.

Mustafa thought for a moment and nodded. "I have not heard that proverb. I like it. It is wise."

"Well if you think I'm a font of wisdom I know one or two privates I'd like you to speak with."

"Ah, you are worried you are not a leader of men? When you hobble on bloody feet yet never stay back when it is time to charge the enemy? Your men see this."

Willoughby didn't know what to say to that so he changed back to the previous subject.

"So once we march to Berlin and I show you the sights, what will you do about the French?"

"God will decide when we will be free of them. We are learning the European way of fighting, which is good, although not so useful in my country as in this one. The war is weakening the French, and that is also good. Perhaps they will be grateful and leave us our country."

"I wouldn't count on it," Willoughby said, wondering if this sort of talk should be reported. He decided that the Colonial troubles of an allied nation weren't part of his remit, and he wouldn't want to cause trouble for Mustafa in any case.

"No, they will probably fight to stay," Mustafa said. "But we will make them leave. God will decide when."

"I see. Let's fight one war at a time, shall we? We are planning another raid tonight."

Mustafa perked up. "To take their new Maxim?"

"Precisely."

"Then here's what I think we should do. I will have some of my men at the far end of my line creep up and snipe at the Germans. This will give you some noise like last time. I will also prepare fifty men at the edge of the copse. When they hear you getting into the fight, they will come up beside the woods and attack the trench there."

"That's sounds excellent," Willoughby said, glad to be getting more help than he had intended on asking for. "Be careful of the Maxim, however."

"We will leave that to you. So the troops do not get mixed up, we will charge directly up the side of the copse and attack the German trench there. It will stop them from coming to support the Maxim from that flank."

"You have a good tactical mind, Mustafa."

The Arab sat a little straighter. "I am from a long line of warriors. My father fought in the Rif and my grandfather was the personal bodyguard of Sultan Moulay Muhammad ibn Abd al-Rahman. And his father before him was personal bodyguard to Sultan Mulai Abd al-Rahman ibn Hisham."

"That's quite a pedigree."

Good Lord, this African has a better lineage than I do!

"Was your father a soldier?" Mustafa asked.

"Um, no, he owns a chain of shops," Willoughby said, embarrassed. He quickly added, "but my uncle was in the army."

"Where did he fight?"

Willoughby felt himself blush. Should he lie? No.

"The Sudan."

Mustafa and the other man who spoke French grinned. Mustafa said something in Arabic and the other men chuckled.

"Nothing personal," Willoughby said. "My uncle always had the highest praise for the courage of the Dervishes."

"Ha! It's no matter, my friend. That's the way of war. One year friends, another year enemies."

"Well I assure you His Majesty's government has no designs on Morocco."

"Your king is wise not to fight Arabs. He leaves that to his enemies."

"Um, yes."

Crawford cut in. "So are we getting our diversion?"

"Yes. I'll give you the details later."

"Are we getting knives too?" Crawford asked.

"Learn French and perhaps you will," Willoughby said.

"I'd like to see you kill a Hun with that thing."

Willoughby wasn't sure if Crawford was being sarcastic or not. Probably he was.

"I have no doubt that you will get your wish, private."

CHAPTER FIFTEEN

Willoughby set his teeth as he heard the soft crackle of the men moving through the underbrush. He hadn't realized how much the rain had dampened the sound of the previous raid. Now, in the still night, every rustle of a leaf, every snap of a twig, sounded like a clarion call to the Germans.

He checked the time on his luminescent watch, a gift from his uncle before he left. Yes, it was five minutes after step off time. Why hadn't Mustafa and the others started their distraction?

He stopped, waving his hand over his head to be noticed in the near-pitch darkness.

The men gathered around.

"We're making too much noise. Crawford, Saunders, and I will go ahead. The rest of you count to a hundred and then follow."

The men nodded. Willoughby smiled. At least these fellows understood not to talk when it wasn't necessary. He knew Crawford would love to grouse about the Arabs but was smart enough not to make noise by asking a question Willoughby couldn't answer.

"Crawford, you're on my left. Saunders, take the right. Stay about five yards to either side of me."

The three set out, moving with care to avoid making any noise.

This is better, Willoughby told himself after they'd made it a few yards in silence, *but what of the others when they start coming up? We'll just have to chance it. At least we're only halfway up. No German will be this far down.*

A burst of gunfire to their front told him he was wrong. Muzzle flares from four rifles flashed in his eyes. Saunders cried out and fell. Willoughby flung himself to the ground. Crawford started firing back.

Willoughby flinched as a muzzle flared right in front of him. It was hard to judge distance in the dark, but it looked close. He fired two rounds at the German and rolled to his right. He heard the sound of running feet behind him, and the distinctive boom of several Lee-Enfields opening up on the Germans.

That's torn it, Willoughby thought, crawling to Saunders as the underbrush pulled at his uniform.

"Oh, Lord no. Oh, no!" Saunders moaned.

The big man lay on his back, clutching his chest. His voice sounded weak and his breathing ragged with a harsh edge to it.

Willoughby slung his rifle and put Saunders' arm around his shoulder. He hauled Saunders to his feet, feeling a jab of pain go through his own aching legs, then half carried, half dragged Saunders down the slope.

"Withdraw!" he called out. "Withdraw!"

A bullet hummed by his head.

"Oh no! Anabelle!" Saunders moaned.

"Quiet!" Willoughby hissed.

"This isn't the right ending," Saunders moaned.

Another bullet cracked a branch just overhead.

It was all Willoughby could do to move Saunders down the slope. Once they bumped into a tree, causing them to fall and making Saunders cry out in pain. Another time an unseen branch scraped Willoughby's face. His legs were hot irons of pain.

The firing tapered off. He heard hurrying feet. A shadow slipped by.

"Help me!" Willoughby whispered.

You fool! What if. . .

His luck held. As the shadow drew close he recognized the service cap of an English soldier.

"I've got him, Corporal," the man said. Willoughby recognized the voice as Private Smith's.

Smith got under Saunders' other arm and together they made their way down the slope. The distinct bark of French Lebel rifles sounded in the distance. Willoughby growled in despair. Mustafa got the timing of the attack wrong. Why?

Of course, we didn't synchronize our watches. What a fool I've been!

At the edge of his hearing he detected the faint sound of many running feet. Mustafa and his men coming to support an attack that was no longer happening.

Willoughby paused, making Smith stumble and tearing another cry of pain from Saunders. He couldn't just leave the Arabs up there, but what could he do? It was already too late and he had to get this man back to the lines.

"Let's go," Willoughby sighed.

The German line erupted in gunfire just as Willoughby and Smith got Saunders back down to the British trench, where they found their entire raiding party reloading.

"Fucking cunts were waiting for us," Crawford griped. "They'll. . ."

His voice trailed off when he spotted the wounded man.

MacDonald hurried to his side. As they laid Saunders on his back, MacDonald opened the shutter on a steel lantern. The pale yellow light from the candle within shone on Saunders. Sweat beaded his pale face. His chest was a mass of blood.

The doctor ripped open the wounded man's shirt. Willoughby winced as he saw the gaping hole bubbling blood. There was no sound except for Saunders' uneven breathing and MacDonald's quick, efficient movements.

MacDonald pulled some cotton wool from his satchel and pressed it against the wound. Saunders put up his hands to his chest.

"Easy now," Willoughby said, gently pushing the hands away.

Saunders reached up his hands again.

"Let him help you," Willoughby said, restraining him.

With surprising strength, Saunders batted him away, felt around, and found the pocket to his shirt. As MacDonald pushed the blood-soaked gauze into the bullet hole and put more on top, Saunders pulled a photograph from his pocket and held it up to the light.

It was of him posed with a woman and a little girl. Willoughby looked from the photo to Saunders. The man's face was graven with pain and longing. His breath became weak, his hand wavered, but he still managed to hold the photograph up to the light.

Then Saunders' face transformed. To Willoughby it seemed like the man was a gas lamp that had suddenly been turned on. The creases of pain smoothed out, the eyes lit up with a sparkle that Willoughby could only call happiness. A smile spread across Saunders' face.

But only for a moment. The eyes glazed over, the smile relaxed into a slack jaw, and the hand fell, smacking the photograph face down into the bloody mess that was once his broad, living chest.

Willoughby stared. Out of the corner of his eye he could see everyone's gaze turn from Saunders to him. The firing uphill grew in intensity. He looked up.

The first man he saw was Crawford.

"We have work to do," Willoughby said. "Assemble a line and engage those men in the woods. Crawford, you come with me. We'll go out into the open to the left and work our way around them. We'll come in at an angle and hit the Maxim. With the firing in the woods they won't be expecting us to come from that direction."

Crawford's eyebrows raised. Slowly he nodded. There was respect in his eyes. Willoughby realized that would have felt wonderful at any other time, but right now a good man lay dead and more good men were up the slope fighting without support.

Willoughby stood. "Let's go."

As the men disappeared once more into the woods, Willoughby and Crawford hurried down the trench about twenty yards and clambered out. Willoughby checked the faint glowing hands of his watch. 0515. All that had happened in a quarter of an hour? Saunders gone in the time it took to fix tea?

Willoughby shook his head and hurried up the slope with Crawford at his side. The pain in his legs was acute. He'd pulled something carrying Saunders' bulk down the hill. He tried to ignore the agony and kept going.

The intense firing of the Lebels and Mausers had fallen silent. Willoughby realized that Mustafa must have called off the attack when he discovered the British weren't there. The sniping in the distance continued unabated, giving them some sound cover.

Rifle fire sounded from the woods to their right. The thicket could be faintly seen as a jagged shadow silhouetted against the dark gray sky.

A bit of predawn light brightened the air. Willoughby forced himself to greater speed.

The firefight in the woods picked up intensity. Occasionally they saw the little point of flame from a muzzle flare through the tangle of branches. The whole German line would be listening to that fight. Eyes would be open but ears would be distracted.

Once they passed the skirmish, they got down and crawled forward.

"We'll try to slip in and bayonet them," Willoughby whispered. "Grab the firing pin and put a couple of rounds into the Maxim for good measure."

"We're not taking it with us?" Crawford asked.

"I haven't the strength and neither of us have the time," Willoughby said. He felt a tug of embarrassment for admitting weakness to someone like Crawford, but they were approaching a trench filled with men who wanted to kill them. Now wasn't the time for posturing.

Rapid gunfire broke out in the distance to their left. Willoughby gritted his teeth. Just the time for Thompson and the others to make a ruckus. They crept forward as quickly as they dared, not wanting to make noise in their rush and not wanting to delay while their friends were getting shot at.

In less than a minute, the sky waxed from a deep gray to a pale milky glow. Willoughby had noticed this phenomenon before. Some trick of topography, some hill over the horizon to the east, meant that the sun below the horizon was kept from shining onto the sky until a certain moment, at which point it came out quite quickly. It still hadn't risen, would not do so for another half hour, but it had illuminated the heavens and diffused its rays through the morning mist.

Oddly, this reduced visibility instead of enhancing it, turning the deep shadows into a uniform haze.

A whispering up ahead made them stop. Willoughby cocked an ear. He recognized German but the words were too low to understand. He touched Crawford on the shoulder and moved off to the right. The private followed, a gray ghost in the mist.

The pair cut along the slope straight for the thicket. They were still firing at each other in there, and Thompson's fight sounded like it was heating up. It kept Willoughby from hearing what the Arabs were doing. The dark bulk of the woods loomed out of the gray haze.

A loud hiss from up the slope. A sparkling light rose into the sky. The field went from dull gray to a bright cloudy white. Willoughby saw in heart-stopping clarity two dead Germans lying in the field a few feet in front of them. Visibility had been so bad he hadn't noticed them before. Now he could have recognized them if he had known them.

Willoughby and Crawford dove for the earth as the German trench roared with gunfire.

CHAPTER SIXTEEN

Major Thompson checked his watch. It was 0455, five minutes until they would set out. He tried to calm his nerves. He didn't mind the fighting so much, it was the waiting that got to him. Of course everyone felt the same, no matter how much they pretended otherwise.

He ran through the plan for the hundredth time. Yes, it was a good one. Simple. Simple plans were the best in these circumstances. Any complicated plan wouldn't last ten minutes in the mist and darkness. And yet he had seen almost as many simple plans die as he had men. When they had marched into the Transvaal they had gone in with a simple plan—defeat a bunch of poorly organized Boer farmers and retake the land for the Empire. The Boers decided to make it less simple.

Well, they had won that war in the end and they'd win this one too. With those machine guns out of the way they stood a good chance of breaking through in the morning.

Only a good chance, not a certain one.

Thompson had a sudden, terrible thought. What if they didn't break through? What if they never broke though? What if, in this war of machine guns and rapid-firing rifles, no charge, no matter how desperate, could make it across these open spaces between the trenches, these spaces owned by no man?

This blood- and rain-drenched slope could become his home for the rest of his life, however short a time that may be.

Five minutes later, as he crawled up the grassy slope at the head of his men, Major Thompson learned something—never polish your boots before going on a raid in the rain. The fresh coat of wax squeaks as it rubs against wet grass. It is a little squeak, a barely audible squeak even to the man making it, but it is a sound.

Thompson wanted no sound. With the rain gone the night had frozen into a tense silence. It was nearly pitch dark but for a pale lightening to gray in the east. There were no shots nearby, no voices. He and twenty men had already made it halfway up to the German trench. Thompson had ordered the men strip off all excess gear and wrap bits of cloth around any metal parts such as belt buckles. He led them slowly, allowing them to pick their movements with care. Still, there were always little noises, like those damned squeaking boots of his.

He focused on moving straight ahead. That was not always easy with the occasional tree or rock to crawl around. He'd already left men in both hollows with orders to give rapid fire straight ahead of their positions once they heard shooting, and continue until they no longer did. If Thompson veered to the left or the right, he and his men might get shot in the back by their own side once the show started.

And he knew they weren't going get into a German trench without their noticing. This would be a localized charge at point blank range. If they could outgun them and gain a section of the trenches, they could kill the crew and wreck the Maxim before the Germans got over their confusion and counterattacked.

A sudden burst of fire to his right made him press himself to the ground. He had ordered the men in the hollows not to shoot if noise came from the direction of the thicket. But he waited for them to shoot anyway, waited for that weakness when a panicked reaction to save one's life overtook the discipline of duty.

It didn't. There was no fusillade from his left and right rear, and mercifully no panic fire from the German trench. The thicket had often been the scene of a nighttime skirmish, so this was nothing new.

But it was at the wrong place and time. The Germans had obviously posted pickets in the woods.

The Mausers and Lee-Enfields broke off quickly. As they fell silent Thompson could hear the Colonials firing further on down the line. Then that, too, tapered away. Thompson waited for several minutes but heard nothing. He signaled to the sergeant behind him and started crawling forward, more slowly than before.

He remembered an area of patchy grass just before the German line at this section. Although he hadn't seen it clearly during his mad charges across it, Thompson remembered it had been eroded, with loose stones and chalk on the surface. It was about ten yards in front of the German trench.

He could just see it ahead now.

The firing in the thicket resumed. Once again he pressed his body to the earth. With one eye he scanned the sky. It had grown noticeably brighter. He felt tempted to look at his watch but that would involve movement. In any case he was committed. Time didn't matter as much as disabling the Maxim and getting out.

The skirmish in the woods continued with no response from either line. Thompson counted to ten, signaled his sergeant, and eased himself forward, setting his teeth in annoyance at the squeak of his boots.

Was that all it took, a squeak? Or was it the resumption of the skirmish in the woods? Had some of the other team been caught in the open, or did a German signaler get panicky? Thompson would never know, but just as he raised himself and started moving forward with his men barely ten yards from the enemy trench, a flare sizzled up into the sky.

Thompson stared at it like a child on Bonfire Night. For a precious second his surprise and the flare's hypnotic brilliance after so many dark hours froze him.

A snap of awareness. A glance at the German line. The light grew and the rocky area in front of him spread out in a pattern of stars and shadow, reaching to the white chalky line of the German trench and its startled, staring faces.

Thompson leapt to his feet and gave them ten rounds rapid. By the second shot he heard the rest of his men doing the same.

Gyrating figures. Upraised hands. Screams. Rapid movement to the side and down. A single muzzle flash from the trench. Thompson charged and reached for a clip at the same time. For five full steps, almost half the distance, there were no shots from the Germans.

Then they recovered. A Mauser banged to his right. Then two more from his left. A head and arm appeared over the parapet directly in front of him just as he pressed the cartridge clip into his Lee-Enfield. As he tossed aside the clip the waxing light made him see with terrible clarity the German pulling back the bolt of his Mauser.

Thompson squeezed off a round. The German flinched, recovered, but by then the Lee-Enfield's sights were lined up and Thompson had snapped back the bolt. The Mauser raised up again. Thompson gave its owner a round in the forehead.

A quick rush and he jumped into the trench. A flurry of bodies on either side landing too. He could hear his support firing on the German lines. Bullets thumped into sandbags, cracked off rocks, or tore cries from the trench's defenders.

Thompson's heart flipped when he realized the Maxim hadn't opened fire. He hadn't even seen it in that mad rushing duel, hadn't had time to look just a bit to the right where he knew it to be. He ran there now, his men falling in behind him.

The gun nest was a simple stretch of trench where the front section had been cut down another foot for the length of a yard. Rocks and sandbags had been placed around the front and sides. In the wavering light of the flare he saw the sickly faces of the two dead crewmen and a smug Tommy standing over them. Private Farley, the last man to the right.

Farley didn't stare long. He turned and grabbed the Maxim, fumbling as he tried to figure out how to remove the firing pin. Thompson strode over, seized the pin, released the catch, and yanked it out.

Just as he did, several shots cracked just down the trench. Thompson pocketed the firing pin.

"Withdraw!"

He grabbed Farley before he could climb out of the trench.

"Help me haul this out into the open."

They slung their rifles and together they got the gun under their shoulders and hefted it out and over the sandbags. Gunfire roared all around them now. As he got out of the trench he could clearly see the muzzle flares of his own men from the two hollows, and a flickering in the trench just by him as the last of his men tried to disengage from the Germans. An Englishman clambered out. Just as he stood, he got shot in the back and fell from sight.

Thompson gave a hurried glance in both directions. Too few had made it out of the trench, barely half his raiding party.

"You!" he called to the man running nearest, "Help Farley carry this as far down as you can."

The man nodded and grabbed the Maxim. The two privates continued down slope.

Thompson turned, pressed another cartridge clip into his rifle, and ran back to the trench.

He made it in time to see another of his men fall. The last two survivors stood back-to-back, pumping bullets down the trench in each direction.

Thompson fired five bullets into one section of the trench, one massed group of shadows muzzles flaring, then turned and gave his last rounds into the other cluster of the enemy.

His men got the message. They flung themselves over the parapet. One came out so close to Thompson that as he rolled onto the grass he kicked Thompson in the shin. All three turned and ran fast and low, sprinting for the British lines for all they were worth. The flare was fading. A Mauser banged and a bullet buzzed by. They ran five yards before another shot came, probably from the same man. Then the Germans recovered and a spattering of fire chased them down the ridge, but by then the flare was guttering out and they had disappeared into the scattered trees and underbrush.

About halfway down they came across the Maxim.

Farley always was a bit lazy.

"Here, help me with this," he ordered the two privates.

The three of them lifted the Maxim and struggled down the slope. Another flare went up just as they were making it back to their lines. The flickering illumination showed a dozen Lee-Enfields pointing at them.

"Hold your fire! It's them!" someone called.

That was a good bit of timing. All thanks to the Germans.

A cheer went up when the men saw the Maxim. Thompson and the others dropped it into the trench with a thud and got inside themselves.

"Top up your rifles, men, and prepare for a counterattack! Cole, are you here?"

"Yes, sir!"

"Do a headcount of the raiding party."

"Yes, sir!"

The flare sank down behind some trees. Another dazzling moment of flickering light and shadows and they were once again plunged into predawn gloom.

Firing continued off to the right. Thompson wondered how Willoughby was faring. Briefly he thought of sending some men to help, but decided that would only add to the confusion. Besides, he needed everyone he had here in case the Germans tried anything.

A low voice a few men away in the trench caught his attention.

"...came back and saved us. You should have seen him blazing away like some Wild West desperado!"

Thompson smiled. Desperate he certainly had been.

CHAPTER SEVENTEEN

Willoughby and Crawford dove behind the pair of dead Germans just as the enemy trench lit up with the flashes of a dozen rifles. Crawford cried out. Willoughby was right behind one of the corpses and felt sure his silhouette melded with the dead man's. He had no idea if Crawford was similarly covered and he didn't dare turn his head to look.

The flare rose to its apex high above, illuminating the whole misty slope in a dreamlike pearly haze. Then it began its slow sputtering descent. As it snuffed out, Willoughby and Crawford leapt up and ran for the woods.

With their eyes dazzled by the flare, neither could see where they were going. Willoughby entangled himself in a bush. From the sound of it Crawford tripped over something and landed flat on his face.

The noise brought another volley from the German trench.

Willoughby tried to extricate himself as quietly as possible.

"Are you all right?" he heard Crawford whisper.

"Yes. You?" Willoughby asked.

"Bastards nipped me in the shoulder. I'm up for it."

Blinking as their eyes adjusted to night vision again, they got up and made their way deeper into the copse. With the exchange of fire continuing downslope, and the occasional blind panic shot from the trench, it didn't matter that they were making noise. No one would hear their movements.

No one except for the man who came crashing through the woods right next to them. Willoughby squinted, desperately trying to see if the vague shadow was friend or foe.

The shadow stopped, moved suddenly as if to raise a weapon. That movement brought his head into a bright patch between two branches, silhouetting his spiked helmet.

Willoughby whipped his *koummya* from its sheath and flung himself on the German. He landed the knife square in his chest but because the blade was curved it didn't plunge straight in. Instead it cut a deep furrow down the man's front.

The German bellowed and swatted Willoughby with an arm the size and strength of a locomotive. Willoughby flew to the side and hit his head on a low branch that stopped him short and almost took him off his feet.

Crawford fired. The German ducked to the side and ran right into Willoughby. Still stunned, Willoughby managed a weak slash down the German's arm that only succeeded in getting his attention.

The German fired from point blank range. Willoughby screamed, but the hasty shot had missed. Willoughby heard a metallic *snick* as the German pulled back the bolt of his Mauser.

With all his strength, Willoughby slashed where he guessed the man's neck would be and felt a jolt as the knife found flesh. The German jerked and gurgled, a sickly sound that made Willoughby's stomach turn. The German slumped to the ground.

"Bloody hell, that's a good 'un." Crawford said next to him.

Willoughby stared at the dead man at his feet, barely visible as a darker shadow amid the gloom. Once when he was twelve he had been visiting his country cousins up in Yorkshire. The groundsman had been cutting the throats of a few sheep to ship to the butchers. The eldest of his cousins, a crude boy a few years older than he, had dared Willoughby to try his hand. Not to be seen as a coward, he had.

It had felt like that, both the cutting and the feeling afterward.

You've killed before now. There's no pleasant way to kill a man, he reasoned. *Those had been different. Firing into a mass of charging Germans or an opposing position, it's not even sure who was my first man. But this. . .*

"You hurt?" Crawford asked. The skirmish in the woods swelled in intensity. Both men ducked.

"No," Willoughby said, taking a deep breath. "Here, put on his greatcoat and helmet. I have an idea."

Crawford did what he was told and the two hurried through the woods toward the German line. Willoughby put Crawford's arm around his shoulder.

"Act like you're hit."

"I am hit! Don't you remember?"

"Well then act like it!"

Crawford slumped into Willoughby's arms, walking forward with a wobbling gait. Willoughby half carried him toward the German line.

"*Eine Verwundete!*" Willoughby called out loud enough to be heard over the gunfire. "*Mir helfen!*"

"This better work," Crawford muttered.

They came out of the thicket into the area the Germans had cleared. The flare was guttering out, but its waning glow as it sank behind the trees cast eerie shadows across the trench. With a start Willoughby saw their own shadows, grossly extended. The spikes atop their *Pickelhaube* covered a yard of ground.

"*Mir helfen!*" Willoughby repeated.

"*Wer bist du?*" someone called out.

They were almost to the trench when there was a loud rustle in the woods behind and two more figures in *Pickelhaube* emerged from the shadows.

"*Halt!*" Came a startled voice from the trench.

"*Nicht schiessen! Ist Hans!*" one of the figures shouted.

The German who called himself Hans turned to peer at Willoughby, who tensed and turned the other way, continuing for the trench. The flare lit up the spaces between the interlaced branches, turning the copse's interior into a latticework of light and shadow. Willoughby made a show of helping Crawford, who contributed with a loud moan that would have sounded reasonably convincing coming from a first-year member of the Oxford Thespian Society if the audience were feeling charitable.

"*Wer bist du?*" The man who had identified himself as Hans asked.

"Now!" Willoughby whispered.

The two Englishmen leapt into the trench. Crawford jammed his bayonet into the neck of the nearest German. Willoughby tried to the same with his man, but only managed to slash him in the face before he landed on the trench bottom, stumbled, and ended up square on his backside with the German looming over him, flailing about and holding his face. Another figure approached from behind him. Willoughby fumbled with his rifle.

Willoughby's first shot made the wounded man fly backwards, entangling himself in his comrade coming to his aid. As the shot man fell, Willoughby fired again. The second German grunted and folded double.

The flare burnt out and Willoughby could see nothing. Remembering the lay of the trench, he emptied his magazine down its length, hoping the narrow confines would allow him to hit what he couldn't see. He only hoped he wasn't wasting his bullets on chalk walls and dead bodies.

"Come on!" Crawford called. He sounded like he was already ten yards down the trench and heading for the Maxim. Willoughby scrambled to his feet and reached for another clip. Two shots fired almost simultaneously in the direction of the Maxim. Someone cried out. Willoughby's chest went cold as he thought he recognized Crawford's voice.

Willoughby thumbed in a five-shot clip. The trench went silent. Willoughby took a careful step forward and retrieved a second clip. He was beginning to be able to see a little now.

"Sie tragen unsere Uniformen!" someone called out.

Blast, they've seen through our ruse.

This cry was followed by another silence, longer than the first.

Willoughby stayed low and crept down the trench.

A short, sharp demand from up ahead. It had been too quick and quiet to tell if it was directed at him or even what language it was.

Willoughby got on one knee, thumbed in another clip, tensing at the sharp click it made, and leveled his rifle.

Two rifles cracked just over the lip of the trench, out toward the woods. A moment later several figures leapt into the trench. Willoughby spotted the outline of a British service cap. The man towered over him, raising his rifle and bayonet to strike.

"It's me!" Willoughby cried.

"Christ! I almost snuffed you," one of the privates said. Willoughby was too terrified to recognize the man by his voice.

"Everyone make it?" Willoughby asked.

"Not sure."

Another flare fizzed into the sky. Everyone got down. As the brilliant ball angled up it cast the trench into deep shadow. A few seconds later the flare rose enough to shine right into the ditch, illuminating everything in a stark light. Willoughby glanced in the direction of the Maxim and saw Crawford gesturing at him. The next moment firing broke out at the far end of the raiding party, directly behind Willoughby.

Willoughby hesitated.

"Follow me!" He hurried toward the Maxim.

The firing behind them grew more intense. Willoughby sensed that only about half his party was behind him, but there was no stopping to check. The Maxim, he remembered, sat in a wider section of trench faced with an embrasure of logs. Good protection from the front but not from the side.

Crawford was finishing off the crew when he arrived. Three Germans and an Englishman lay in a heap, with Crawford putting his bayonet through the chest of one bloodied German already on the ground.

He turned to Willoughby.

"Don't they teach you to be punctual at Oxford?"

"Don't they teach manners in prison?"

"Oi! Kills a few Germans and puts on the airs of a general!"

Willoughby grinned. Why this layabout's approval mattered to him was a mystery he didn't have time to solve. He was about to grab the Maxim's firing pin when a burst of Lebel fire sounded just down the line.

"Mustafa's come back!"

"About time, the bloody darkie," one of the privates said.

"Shut up and cover the other end of the trench," Willoughby ordered.

Another man came hurrying from that direction. "They're gone!"

"What?"

"The Huns bolted!"

Willoughby looked around. It was a shame not to take advantage of this, but he couldn't see how to manage it. The Germans and the Moroccans were heavily engaged by the sound of it, but by the time he made it back to the British line and tried to get the Yorkshires to come up the entire situation might change.

Crawford pulled out the Maxim's firing pin with a snap. Two of the other men tore out the hose from the water cooling system, tossed it into the darkness, tipped the machine gun over and pumped several rounds into its works.

"Time to go, men," Willoughby said.

"Congratulations lads!" Crawford shouted. "We've taken two of their guns in as many nights!"

Willoughby chuckled as he and the others ran back downhill. His legs didn't hurt anymore. He saw Crawford stumble.

"What's the matter?" Willoughby asked.

"That shoulder wound's got me a bit lightheaded, and my side's opened up. Magnetic MacDonald didn't patch it up well enough."

"Magnetic who?" Willoughby asked, putting Crawford's arm around his shoulder and letting the private put some of his weight on him.

"The medical man. He attracts shells and bullets like a lodestone."

"You're one to talk; you've been wounded twice in the past twenty-four hours."

"You would be too, if you were in the thick of it."

"I beg your pardon?"

Crawford let out a little laugh. They were passing through a few bushes and trees that offered some cover.

"That was quite the acting job you put on," Crawford said. His voice sounded winded and he leaned more on Willoughby. The corporal tried to pick up the pace.

"I was in the Oxford Thespian Society."

"Thespian? You mean those, heh, strong girls?"

"What are you nattering on about?"

"Oh nothing. I misunderstood, sir."

"Don't sir me. If you want to show me the respect I'm due, stop bleeding on me."

CHAPTER EIGHTEEN

20 September

With both Maxims captured or disabled, the British attack that morning should have pushed the Germans back over the ridge and forced them to continue their retreat to Berlin.

That didn't happen.

Before the British Expeditionary Force could make a big push, the Germans attacked first. They started with a storm of artillery fire against the Moroccan position, followed by a massed charge. The Colonials, exhausted by being on the line since the beginning of the battle and with little support from their high command, buckled. This left the Yorkshire right exposed, and soon the Germans swept through the copse and rolled up the Yorkshire line.

The Germans made it all the way to the Durham Light Infantry to their left, who managed to hold on until the Sherwood Foresters rushed in and stabilized the situation. By the time the Ox and Bucks made it uphill, the Germans were withdrawing back to their trenches. The situation was stabilized but the big British push was cancelled.

All that trouble for nothing, thought Private Timothy Crawford, rummaging amid the German corpses looking for valuables. One arm was in a sling and the work was going too slowly for his liking, although he'd nicked three good watches already.

Two Maxims in as many nights, thought Corporal Hugh Willoughby as he puffed out his chest and breathed in the morning air.

Lucky bastard, he's getting out of here, thought Captain George MacDonald as he saw his men carry away Mustafa, who had gunshot wound in his shoulder. He made a mental note to tell Willoughby his friend had survived.

All that trouble for nothing, thought Major Neville Thompson as he clutched the back of Sergeant Harry Kempthorne's motorcycle and was once again driven to Battalion HQ in Pont-Arcy.

Well, let's try to make something out of nothing.

Kempthorne dropped him off at HQ and Thompson found his way to the map room, where Lieutenant-Colonel Nesbitt stood alone looking down at a large map spread on the table. Thompson noted that it wasn't a map of the Aisne River valley, but rather a large-scale map of northeastern France.

Nesbitt looked up when Thompson entered the room.

"Ah Thompson, there you are. How does it feel to lead a company with a proper designation?"

Thompson saluted. "I and the men have gotten used to being E Company, sir."

Neville chuckled. "Well, you're A Company now, and you'll stay A Company. I've had word from the RAMC. Lawson is in a bad way. Will be on indefinite sick leave back in England."

"I'm sorry to hear that, sir," Thompson said.

Poor fellow. At least he's out of it.

"I read your report," Lieutenant-Colonel Nesbitt said. "Quite a little surprise you gave the Hun. Sherry?"

The officer lifted a bottle and a glass.

"Thank you, sir."

Nesbitt poured two full glasses, put the bottle away in a cabinet, and offered a glass to Thompson.

"To the King," Nesbitt declared.

"To the King."

They drank. Nesbitt slugged down half his glass in one go. Thompson took a large enough sip to be polite.

"The division is moving north," Nesbitt announced.

"Is it, sir?"

"Yes, as you know the Hun have been digging in all the way to the Channel. We're gathering with several other divisions further north for a breakthrough."

"I didn't know that, sir. The men are ready, sir,"

"I have every faith that they are. Your company has caught my eye, Thompson, and the eyes of more than one man in Divisional HQ." Nesbitt's face darkened. "The Huns are more resilient than we thought. They'll give us a hard fight. Once we break through their lines they'll probably fall back and dig in again, most likely at the Somme. This war may last well into the spring. I daresay we'll need your raiding skills once or twice before we reach Berlin."

"E Company is ready, sir."

Neville chuckled and shook his head, turning back to the cabinet to refill his glass with sherry.

"Sending out a regiment with five companies, what is this man's army coming to! Well I hope as A Company you fight as well as you did when you were E Company."

E Company took those Maxims. We're still E Company, Thompson corrected him silently.

"We'll endeavor to do our best, sir," he said out loud.

"You'll have your chance," Nesbitt said, draining his glass and setting it down on a spot on the map. "We won't be staying here. Trying to break through on this ground is too costly. Some new regiments will be replacing us and we'll join a big push further up the line. We're gathering to break through here, at a town called Ypres."

Thompson looked at the dot on the map. It meant nothing to him.

"Yes, Thompson, the high command wants a breakthrough and by God we'll give it to them. Mark my word, Thompson, the name Ypres will go down in history as the place where we won the war."

Continue reading for a sneak peek of Trench Raiders Book Two: Digging In, *and a historical note about the Oxs and Bucks at the Battle of the Aisne.*

Digging In
Trench Raiders Book Two
CHAPTER ONE

29 October 1914

What a miserable excuse for a trench.

Major Neville Thompson watched Company E of the 2/4 Oxfordshire and Buckinghamshire Light Infantry slop the mud out of waterlogged shell craters and connect them with a pathetic ditch that looked more like the drainage system for a country road than a defense to keep the Germans from taking Ypres.

His men were filthy, tired, and increasingly despondent. He looked at those haggard faces, their youthful features etched in deep lines after two weeks of hard fighting on the River Aisne and two weeks of hard marching before that. At the Aisne it had been the British trying to break through and march on Berlin. That had ended in failure and Thompson had lost half his men, so they and the rest of the division had shifted north to the last bit of unoccupied Belgium, only to find the Germans had got here first and were preparing an offensive.

Artillery fire thundered along the line for miles to his right and left. At the moment the Oxs and Bucks weren't getting any, and so the men feverishly tried to deepen the trenches and fortify them with sandbags. A few Belgian peasants—squat, solid men who hadn't yet fled their homes—lent a hand.

Thompson peered out across the open fields, dull yellow and brown under a leaden sky. At least they had a good field of fire for more than a quarter of a mile to that line of trees. The Germans were positioned behind them. He could just make out a few of their spiked *Pickelhaube* helmets through the trees when he looked through his binoculars. He couldn't tell if the Germans were digging in too. It didn't matter. The

British Expeditionary Force was outnumbered and far too weak to make an assault. The French to their north and south were still trying, and dying by the thousands. The British didn't have thousands to spare.

A shrill whirr made him leap into the trench, splatting face-first into the mud just as a loud bang assaulted his ears. Another came, and another. Everyone squished themselves into the mud, all but for a few sentries whose grim task was to keep watch while everyone else took cover. Bitter experience had taught Thompson to expect to lose two or three sentries a day.

A scream from his right told him that today's third had just been hit.

There was nothing Thompson could do but keep his head down and weather the storm. Several bangs burst in front and behind the shallow trench. A shell splinter sent up a spray of mud close to his left. He glanced at the man next to him and saw he was unhurt. Over the noise, however, he could hear a sustained wailing. Someone had been hit badly. Probably had a limb cut off. Men with belly or chest wounds only made weak little coughs, and a head wound kept them from making any sound at all. Thompson had become an expert in the sounds of pain.

Captain Thomas Cole crawled over to him, barely recognizable under a fresh coating of mud.

"Messenger came in just before the bombardment started, sir. The Second Worcestershires on our left have beaten back a charge."

"And they were shelled just like this half an hour ago," Thompson finished his second-in-command's sentence.

"Yes, sir," Cole replied.

"Go along the line and tell the men to get ready," Thompson ordered, but Cole was already crawling away to do just that.

Thompson nodded as he watched his second-in-command go. A good man. All his men were good men, but they were utterly worn out, part of a thin line of good men, far too few, trying to keep back a vastly larger force of Germans from breaking through and sweeping over Belgium and northern France.

There's no chance we can hold off their assaults with this little trench. No barbed wire, barely enough shells for the artillery, too few men, no sleep, and hardly any reinforcements except for these Belgian farmers and their antiquated fowling pieces. This can't work.

But it had to work. If the Germans broke through, they'd take the railway nexus at Ypres and push on west to take the Channel ports all the way to Calais. Belgium would be lost, the British Expeditionary Force would be cut off from reinforcements and supplies, and the French would most likely sue for peace. It was hold or lose the war.

And Thompson had buried far, far too many men to lose the war.

Thompson peered over the lip of the trench and saw he was about to lose more.

A grey line of Germans was emerging from the woods.

CHAPTER TWO

Corporal Aubrey Bennet had never seen a German before. He peered along the sights of his Vickers, watching as the serried grey line approached.

Bennet had just come in from England as part of the reserve, meeting up with his Ox and Bucks pals at the Ypres train station the day before. It was his first time out of the country, his first time in war, and the first time he was about to shoot his machine gun at something other than a wooden target.

Puffs of white smoke flowered above the German line, white stems of shrapnel arching out from all sides. Germans fell by ones and tens, but still they advanced. The Royal Artillery weren't going to stop this charge. Bennet didn't need to be a veteran to know that.

Glancing at Bill Reed, his loader, he saw the man was ready. All they had left to do was to wait until the Germans had closed a bit more distance. Half a minute at most, then he'd give his own back for losing Saunders.

A good man, Saunders. They always used to go to the pictures at the Bicester Playhouse together. Saunders loved the pictures, even dreamed about making some himself. Saunders had come out before him and got killed in the fighting on the Aisne. The Huns were going to pay for taking his pal.

He watched the grey line advance. Directly in front of him he could see an officer waving his sword to urge on his men. Maybe it was that bastard who had killed Saunders, or maybe it was that buck Hun to his left. The monster was seven feet if he was an inch. Didn't matter. He'd kill them all.

Strange, this. Three days before, he'd been sitting at the table with Emily and the children and his Ma. Emily had cooked a big going-away dinner, bought a whole chicken from Bicester market with all the trimmings. It had been like Christmas without the snow.

A few yards more and he'd fire.

That had been a grand time. And now he was here. It didn't seem real.

Five more seconds. Ellsworth and Hedges on his right were ready with their Vickers too. Ellsworth was a good shot, but not as good as him. Bennet always got the top marks on the firing range.

One more second.

Now.

He took his finger off the trigger guard, rested it on the trigger, and squeezed. The Vickers rattled to life. From down the shaking sights he could see a blur of air, his bullets spewing out at 450 rounds a minute. Through the blur he saw men fall like rows of wheat to a scythe. The officer with the sword went down almost at once, as did a great clump of men directly behind him. The buck Hun, biggest of the lot, crumpled like paper. And then there was no one there, just a hole and clear air all the way to the tree line. For a second he stared at it in awe.

Bennet remembered himself and eased the Vickers to the left, letting out a steady stream of bullets along the German line. Everywhere that blur touched, men fell. He hoped Ellsworth was getting the Huns to the right, but he didn't dare look away to check. No need to worry. Ellsworth would keep his head.

He kept firing. Down down down they went in a regular line. By some freak of the mechanism a clump of men was skipped, suddenly marooned in the great empty space he had created. Bennet edged the Vickers back and tore through them. Three seconds and they were all gone.

He moved the machine gun to the left again and kept firing. The rat-tat-tat of his Vickers stopped, the blur disappeared, and all he saw was the field, the men writhing in the distance, and the line rent with holes yet still advancing.

He glanced at Reed, who was already fitting another belt into the mechanism. Bennet aligned his eye with the sights again.

"Ready!" Reed's shout was barely audible over the ringing in his ears.

Bennet picked up where he had left off. The Huns were closer now and went down faster as more of his bullets struck home. He saw each one clear as day. Each blossom of blood on a chest or a head, each gyrating arm, each flailing fall.

A few were missed, running alone or in pairs where once they had run in a dense pack. He ignored them and fired where the line was thickest, where his bullets would be most efficient.

Another belt done, another 250 rounds fired. Reed loaded up again and Bennet saw that the wave of men was all but gone now. He spared a glance at Ellsworth's portion and found the lad had done well. What had once been a solid mass was now a scattering of men, spread out no thicker than a football team coming up the pitch. One by one these survivors were picked off by the riflemen. The artillery had stopped firing. There was no need.

Another wave emerged from the woods, thicker than the first. Bennet waited until they were in range and mowed them down like the one before. It took three belts this time, 750 rounds, before that wave broke. Bennet expended a fourth belt tearing through clumps of Huns as they fled for the woods. The riflemen got most of the rest.

The Huns didn't send a third wave.

He could hear the men cheering, their voices sounding muffled and distant to his battered eardrums. Reed, efficient as ever, loaded another belt.

Bennet looked out over the mass of grey humps. Some writhed. A few crawled painfully back towards the woods. Most lay still. He heard Timothy Crawford's voice ring out.

"Good job, lads, we did it!"

No, I did it. Me and Ellsworth.

He glanced over at his fellow machine gunner. Ellsworth was looking right at him, eyes glazed, face pale, mouth slack.

Bennet blinked and looked away.

"Got them for you, Saunders," he whispered.

The words came out dry and lifeless.

CHAPTER THREE

All Sergeant Hugh Willoughby wanted to do was sleep. He had been hunkered down in this mere scrape of a trench all day and all the previous night. Before that it had been marching, and the day before that more marching. There had been short rest breaks, of course, but between the constant shelling and his new duties as a sergeant for his platoon, he doubted he had got more than three hours of sleep in the last three days.

Not that the men were much better off.

They were digging again, slinging mud out of their waterlogged ditch as shells burst all around. They had given up hiding from every bombardment. To do that would mean no work would get done. Instead they only lay low if the bombardment got bad. Right now their line was being hit with only one or two shrapnel shells every minute. Nothing to get fidgety about.

It was strange to think that only three months before he had been a shy student at Oxford, jumping when a door slammed and never thinking he'd hear a shot fired in anger, let alone fire one himself. But he had fired, and he had killed.

How many? At least five, probably more. It was hard to keep count and probably best not to. Some men counted out of a sense of bravado. Willoughby felt no bravado. He just wanted to do his duty and get through this alive. He'd probably killed one or two more in that last charge, but it was hard to tell with those two Vickers crews blazing away.

"Shit," Private Timothy Crawford grumbled as he slung mud next to him.

"What?" Willoughby asked.

The bang of a nearby shell made Crawford's answer unintelligible.

"What was that?" Willoughby repeated.

"The rain's picking up."

"Oh, so it is. I thought you were about to tell me something important."

"Well, breakfast is late, is that important?"

"Yes it is, and yes, it is."

"Er wot?"

"I'd like some breakfast too."

Crawford's face lit up. "Send me back, sergeant sir, I know the cook and can get him running."

"Don't 'sergeant sir' me. You just want to linger in the rear."

Willoughby could always tell when Crawford was up to something because he'd act respectfully. If he really wanted something he could even manage a "sir."

Crawford put on a hurt face. "I'm no lingerer."

"Not in a fight you're not. But standing in a watery ditch getting shelled isn't exactly your cup of tea."

"If you want tea, sir—"

"Dig."

They dug in silence for a while, only stopping their work to duck at the occasional close hit. At last Crawford threw his entrenching tool down in disgust and leaned against the wall.

"I'm dying for a fag," he sighed.

Willoughby pulled a cigar out of his pocket. Crawford's eyes widened.

"Where did you get that?"

"Remember those Belgians that gave us all sorts of gifts on the march?"

"Of course I do. If it weren't for them I'd have been out of fags a week ago."

"This was from them. I'll trade it to you if you have any chocolate left."

A grin spread across Crawford's face. "You're learning, you are."

Crawford pulled out two pieces of chocolate and offered the smaller one to Willoughby. The sergeant raised his eyebrow and Crawford quickly switched the little one for the big one.

"Both pieces, if you please. This is my last cigar, and scarcity always raises the price. Rule of economics, don't you know."

Crawford grunted, handed him the chocolate and took the cigar. He gazed at it lovingly for a moment and passed it under his nose. Then he paused and looked up at Willoughby.

"The last one? Wait, why don't I ever see you smoking?"

"I don't smoke. It's bad for the health."

Crawford barked out a laugh. "Bad for the health?" he gestured at the waterlogged trench around them, and at the German trench in the distance. A shell burst not far off. "Bad for the health?"

Ten minutes later Captain Cole came squishing down the trench. "Breakfast break! Open up some tins of bully beef, lads. The kitchen got hit by a heavy one and is smashed to smithereens."

"What, no tea?" Willoughby asked. No hot breakfast was bad enough, but a morning in the rain without tea was unthinkable.

"No scones either, I'm afraid," Cole said.

A few men chuckled. Willoughby felt himself blush. Cole had been Major Thompson's gardener in civilian life, and only the upside down world of war could get such a man to speak to Willoughby, an Oxford student, in such tones. Of course Cole was a veteran of the Boer War, but that didn't mean the man should forget himself in front of his betters.

Willoughby wondered if perhaps he should have taken a commission when he'd been offered one instead of trying to prove himself by working his way up the ranks.

He tossed his shovel aside with contempt and sat down. Rummaging around his pack he found a tin of bully beef. Crawford sat down next to him with a tin of his own.

"No tea, no hot food, no anything," Crawford grumbled, using his bayonet to open his tin. It popped open with a hiss and a terrible stench.

"Fuck!" Crawford shouted. The contents were green. "My morning starts with an hour of digging and a nose full of bully gas."

The private tossed the tin out of the trench.

"Gangrene in a tin," Willoughby said with a smile, handing him another one.

Crawford looked at it suspiciously, turning it over in his hands.

"'Fray Bentos,'" he read. "'Product of Uruguay'. Oi, what we getting foreign beef for?"

"Probably because there aren't enough cattle in England to feed the army."

"There would be if they fed us something different once in a while."

"At least we're not eating horse like the Belgians," one of the other privates said. On their march up to the line, one of the horses had broken a leg and had to be shot. As soon as it was dead, the local villagers had rushed out with knives and cut up the animal. The looks on those starving, desperate faces had affected them all.

Crawford held up an unsavory chunk of meat on the end of his bayonet. "How can you be sure we're not?"

A bunch of the men laughed.

Willoughby looked at the Belgian peasants who had been helping them dig. They were young boys or old men and sat in a little group, sharing out a meager portion of bread and cheese.

Willoughby addressed his platoon. "Men, pull out an extra can of bully beef each and give it to the Belgians."

One of the new arrivals piped up, "With respect, sergeant, general orders state that we're not supposed to give out—"

"Shut your pie hole and pull out that bully beef!" Crawford barked.

The man cringed and did as he was told. Willoughby smiled. Crawford would make a good NCO if his service record didn't keep him from getting promoted. Willoughby gathered a tin from each man and went over to the Belgians.

"Here you go," he addressed them in French. "Thank you for helping."

One grey-haired farmer, whose broad face was embellished with a thick handlebar moustache, nodded and replied, "It is the least we can do. I wish I was young enough to join my son in the ranks. All the men of fighting age are in the line."

"We're still fighting age!" another elderly farmer said, brandishing a shotgun. "Just tell your machine gunners to let some of the Bosche get close enough and I'll show you what this can do."

The first man laughed. "Ignore Renaud. He can't hit a partridge if it's sitting on his own front fence. I know because I've seen."

A few of the other Belgians laughed. Renaud frowned. "You be quiet! You'll see what I can do!"

"Well, a warrior needs to keep up his strength," Willoughby said, "So eat up, *monsieur*."

Renaud scowled. "Don't condescend to me, young man. You have come over from England to fight and we're grateful for it, but your country hasn't been touched by war. You haven't had your homes burned, seen civilians shot in the street, seen. . ."

Renaud let his sentence trail off. Willoughby realized the old fellow was too dignified to go on. There had been other crimes too. Women outraged, children bayoneted. It was in all the English papers. Willoughby took on a soothing tone.

"We'll make the Germans pay. The Belgians and the English and all their allies will make them pay."

Renaud grunted and fumbled with his tin. A boy sitting next to him grinned.

"Not that way, grandfather, this way."

The boy took the tin from the old man, pulled the key out from the side, inserted it into a groove at the top and unwound the thin metal lid.

Willoughby struggled through the mud back to his men.

"His men." He couldn't believe it. He had joined the war as a private. With his social position he could have joined as a subaltern, he could have had Cole's place as Thompson's second-in-command by now, yet he had ignored his father's and his recruiting officer's objections and enlisted as a private. His friends and family still didn't understand. When they badgered him as to why, he simply said that he wanted to earn his stripes.

As if anyone didn't in this war! Even Major Thompson was out on the firing line day in and day out, and on the Aisne had led charges against machine guns. No, it hadn't been to prove himself, although that had been part of it, it had been to keep himself from being a coward.

He'd always been the weak one at school. Oh, physically he had been decent enough despite his bookish inclinations, but he'd never been good at games and being in the same room as one of the school toughs made him want to curl up and blow away. He'd joined the Oxford University Reserves in the hopes that it would toughen him up, assuming that there would never be a war serious enough for him to be needed. Wrong on both counts.

The thought of coming under fire had terrified him. What he feared most of all, though, was shirking, those daily bits of cowardice he'd seen in so many men. The recruiting officer, a brutish Scottish bastard, had even hinted as much when he offered him a post in the Army Postal Service. Imagine going through the war as a postman! The very thought made him flush with embarrassment, tinged with self-loathing at the knowledge that he had been tempted. If he had come in as a subaltern there would have been a thousand ways to hide in the rear, a thousand little temptations, so he had enlisted as a private and forced himself to be brave.

It had worked, after a fashion. He'd done things most men only read about in the illustrated papers. He'd earned his way up to corporal and then sergeant, and now he was in command of a platoon of twenty men who, he thought and earnestly hoped, respected him. Most of them were pub bruisers like Crawford and Black, men who would have scared the daylights out of him three months ago. They still did at times, but he had more important things to be scared of.

"Here they come!" one of the sentries called.

Willoughby poked his head over the parapet. Germans were swarming through the line of trees on the opposite side of the field.

Time to prove himself again.

Digging In *is now available as an ebook anywhere ebooks are sold.*

Want to read some of my books for free?

If you sign up for my newsletter[1], *Sean's Travels and Tales*, you get TWO FREE EBOOKS—the historical mystery *Tangier Bank Heist* and the post-apocalyptic science fiction *Radio Hope*. In addition, each monthly issue features a short story or travel article, a coupon for a free or discounted book, and updates on future projects. How cool is that? You can subscribe using this link[2]. Your email will not be shared with anyone else.

---

1. https://books.bookfunnel.com/seanmclachlan

2. https://books.bookfunnel.com/seanmclachlan

About the Author

Sean McLachlan worked for ten years as an archaeologist in Israel, Cyprus, Bulgaria, and the United States before becoming a full-time writer. He is the author of numerous fiction and nonfiction books, which are listed on the following pages. When he's not writing, he enjoys hiking, reading, traveling, and, most of all, teaching his son about the world. He divides his time between Madrid, Oxford, and Cairo.

To find out more about Sean's work and travels, visit him at his website[1] or blog[2], and feel free to friend him on Goodreads[3] and Facebook[4]. And don't forget to nab two free ebooks by subscribing to his newsletter[5]! Your email won't be shared with anyone.

---

1. https://www.seanmclachlan.net/
2. http://midlistwriter.blogspot.com
3. http://www.goodreads.com/author/show/623273.Sean_McLachlan
4. https://www.facebook.com/writersean
5. https://books.bookfunnel.com/seanmclachlan

Fiction by Sean McLachlan

Trench Raiders (Trench Raiders Book One)

September 1914: The British Expeditionary Force has the Germans on the run, or so they think.

After a month of bitter fighting, the British are battered, exhausted, and down to half their strength, yet they've helped save Paris and are pushing towards Berlin. Then the retreating Germans decide to make a stand. Holding a steep slope beside the River Aisne, the entrenched Germans mow down the advancing British with machine gun fire. Soon the British dig in too, and it looks like the war might grind down into deadly stalemate.

Searching through No-Man's Land in the darkness, Private Timothy Crawford of the Oxfordshire and Buckinghamshire Light Infantry finds a chink in the German armor. But can this lowly private, who spends as much time in the battalion guardhouse as he does on the parade ground, convince his commanding officer to risk everything for a chance to break through?

Available in electronic and print editions!

Digging In (Trench Raiders Book Two)

October 1914: The British line is about to break.

After two months of hard fighting, the British Expeditionary Force is short of men, ammunition, and ideas. With their line stretched to the breaking point, aerial reconnaissance spots German reinforcements massing for the big push. As their trenches are hammered by a German artillery battery, the men of the Oxfordshire and Buckinghamshire Light Infantry come up with a desperate plan—a daring raid behind enemy lines to destroy the enemy guns and give the British a chance to stop the German army from breaking through.

Available in electronic and print editions!

No Man's Land (Trench Raiders Book Three)

No Man's Land—a hellscape of shell craters and dead bodies. Soldiers have fought over it, charged across it, and bled on it for a year of grueling war, but neither side has dominated it.

Until now.

An elite German raiding party is passing through No Man's Land every night, attacking the British trenches at will. The Oxfordshire and Buckinghamshire Light Infantry need to reassert control over their front lines.

So the exhausted men of Company E decide to set a trap, a nighttime ambush in the middle of No Man's Land, where any mistake can be fatal. But the few surviving veterans are leading recruits who have only been in the trenches for two weeks. Mistakes are inevitable.

Available in electronic and print editions!

Christmas Truce

Christmas 1914

In the cold, muddy trenches of the Western Front, there is a strange silence. As the members of a crack English trench raiding team enjoy their first day of peace in months, they call out holiday greetings to the men on the German line. Soon both sides are fraternizing in No Man's Land.

But when the English recognize some enemy raiders who only a few days before launched a deadly attack on their position, can they keep the peace through the Christmas truce?

Available in electronic and print editions!

Warpath into Sonora

Arizona 1846

Nantan, a young Apache warrior, is building a name for himself by leading raids against Mexican ranches to impress his war chief, and the chief's lovely daughter. But there is one thing he and all other Apaches fear—a ruthless band of Mexican scalp hunters who slaughter entire villages.

Nantan and his friends have sworn to fight back, but they are inexperienced, and led by a war chief driven mad with a thirst for revenge. Can they track their tribe's worst enemy into unknown territory and defeat them?

Available in electronic and print editions!

The Case of the Purloined Pyramid (The Masked Man of Cairo Book One)

An ancient mystery. A modern murder.

Sir Augustus Wall, a horribly mutilated veteran of the Great War, has left Europe behind to open an antiquities shop in Cairo. But Europe's troubles follow him as a priceless inscription is stolen and those who know its secrets start turning up dead. Teaming up with Egyptology expert Moustafa Ghani, and Faisal, an irritating street urchin he just can't shake, Sir Wall must unravel an ancient secret and face his own dark past.

Available in electronic and print editions!

The Case of the Shifting Sarcophagus (The Masked Man of Cairo Book Two)

An Old Kingdom coffin. A body from yesterday.

Sir Augustus Wall had seen a lot of death. From the fields of Flanders to the alleys of Cairo, he'd solved several murders and sent many men to their grave. But he's never had a body delivered to his antiquities shop encased in a 5,000 year-old coffin.

Soon he finds himself fighting a vicious street gang bent on causing national mayhem while his assistant, Moustafa Ghani, faces his own enemies in the form of colonial powers determined to ruin him. Throughout all this runs the street urchin Faisal. Ignored as usual, dismissed as usual, he has the most important fight of all.

Available in electronic and print editions!

The Case of the Golden Greeks (The Masked Man of Cairo Book Three)

They thought the case was solved.

When an eminent Egyptologist is murdered giving a lecture in front of a packed hall, Cairo's chief of police quickly rounds up those responsible.

Or at least some of them.

Sir Augustus Wall, antiquities dealer and amateur sleuth, knows there's more to the crime than it seems. With little to go on but an exotic murder weapon, a map of a desert oasis, and some gilded Greek mummies, he sets out across the Sahara with his assistant Moustafa Ghani and the street urchin Faisal, who is the only person to have seen the killer's face. They soon find themselves in the midst of international intrigue on Egypt's remote border with Libya.

Can they discover what mystery lies beneath Bahariya Oasis?

Available in electronic and print editions!

The Case of the Karnak Killer (The Masked Man of Cairo Book Four)

A scandal in America. A murder in Cairo.

Sir Augustus Wall, antiquities dealer and amateur sleuth, is hired to track down a blackmailer who threatens the reputation of an American millionaire. When blackmail turns to murder, he must travel up the Nile by steamboat to find the killer.

Joining him are Faisal, a street urchin who makes himself equally useful and troublesome; Heinrich Schäfer, a leading Egyptologist; and Jocelyn Montjoy, an adventurous woman who has captured his heart.

But complications set in before the hunt even begins. Unwelcome fellow passengers threaten to derail the investigation, and Augustus has fallen out with his right-hand man, Moustafa Ghani. Can a new team of investigators help him solve his most challenging case yet?

Available in electronic and print editions!

The Case of the Asphyxiated Alexandrian (The Masked Man of Cairo Book 5)

A mysterious murder. A lost pharaoh.

Sir Augustus Wall came to Egypt to escape his old life, but when a comrade from the trenches is found murdered in a Cairo hotel, Augustus realizes his past has finally caught up.

Now he must discover the reason for the baffling murder, leading him and his friends Moustafa and Faisal on a dangerous hunt for the most sought-after treasure in Egypt.

The long-awaited fifth book in the Masked Man of Cairo series sees the trio on their greatest adventure yet!

Available in electronic and print editions!

The Case of the Dastardly Djinn (A Masked Man of Cairo Prequel)

A homeless boy. A hunted girl.

Cairo, 1917. In a city plagued by poverty and war, ten-year-old Faisal begs and steals to survive, hiding at night from the things that prowl after dark. The nimblest and most clever of the street boys, he's terrified of the unseen spirits he's convinced haunt the ancient city.

But when he discovers a girl his age left homeless by a terrible tragedy, Faisal decides to do what no one ever did for him—help. With no shelter and facing the many dangers of Cairo's darkened streets, Faisal's loyalties are tested when together they uncover a criminal ring more sinister than his worst superstitions.

This prequel to the Masked Man of Cairo mystery adventure series will thrill new readers and long-time fans alike!

A portion of the proceeds from this book will go to help Egyptian street children.

Available in electronic and print editions!

Tangier Bank Heist: An Interzone Mystery

Right after the war, Tangier was the craziest town in North Africa. Everything was for sale and the price was cheap. The perverts came for the flesh. The addicts came for the drugs. A whole army of hustlers and grifters came for the loose laws and free flow of cash and contraband.

So why was I here? Because it was the only place that would have me. Besides, it was a great place to be a detective. You got cases like in no other place I'd ever been, and I'd been all over. Cases you couldn't believe ever happened. Like when I had to track down the guy who stole the bank.

No, he didn't rob the bank, he stole it.

Here's how it happened . . .

Available in electronic and print editions!

Three Passports to Trouble (Interzone Mystery Book 2)

Back in the days when Tangier was an International Zone, the city was full of refugees. People fleeing Stalin. People fleeing Franco. People fleeing the Nuremburg Trials. Tangier offered a safe haven from the chaos of Europe.

The International Council had to keep a delicate balance, tolerating everything from anti-capitalist agitators to Germans with murky pasts. It was the only way to keep the peace, and it worked.

Until an anarchist was found dead with a fascist dagger in his chest.

And I got stuck with the case just when I had to smuggle a couple of Party operatives out of town.

Available in electronic and print editions!

Flight to Fez (Interzone Mystery Book Three)

Only in Tangier could a literary event turn into a murder scene.

I'm "Shorty" MacAllister, private detective. I've investigated all sorts of crazy cases in this lawless town, tracking down con men and Nazi fugitives, anarchists and bank robbers, all the while running my own secret angle.

But I never thought that when I went to hear my friend Jane Bowles read her latest story I'd end with a murdered man in my lap, and an old war buddy getting pinned with the crime.

After that, things got a whole lot more complicated.

Available in electronic and print editions!

A Winter Murder in Berlin (The Berlin Murders Book One)

The voyage of a lifetime turns into a nightmare.

When Katherine Schmidt sails for Europe in late 1929, she looks forward to a year of carefree travel thanks to an unexpected inheritance. But when a companion on her steamer is murdered and she becomes a suspect, she needs to find the real killer before the police close in. Now she must delve into Weimar Berlin's decadent nightlife and radical politics in order to clear her name.

Can an innocent young woman from Missouri outwit fascists, communists, and the denizens of Berlin's notorious shadow world?

Available in electronic and print editions!

Radio Hope (Toxic World Book One)

In a world shattered by war, pollution and disease...

A gunslinging mother longs to find a safe refuge for her son.

A frustrated revolutionary delivers water to villagers living on a toxic waste dump.

The assistant mayor of humanity's last city hopes he will never have to take command.

One thing gives them the promise of a better future—Radio Hope, a mysterious station that broadcasts vital information about surviving in a blighted world. But when a mad prophet and his army of fanatics march out of the wildlands on a crusade to purify the land with blood and fire, all three will find their lives intertwining, and changing forever.

Available in print and electronic editions!

Refugees from the Righteous Horde (Toxic World Book Two)

When you only have one shot, you better aim true.

In a ravaged world, civilization's last outpost is reeling after fighting off the fanatical warriors of the Righteous Horde. Sheriff Annette Cruz becomes New City's long arm of vengeance as she sets off across the wildlands to take out the cult's leader. All she has is a sniper's rifle with one bullet and a former cultist with his own agenda. Meanwhile, one of the cult's escaped slaves makes a discovery that could tear New City apart...

Available in electronic and print editions!

We Had Flags (Toxic World Book Three)

A law doesn't work if everyone breaks it.

For forty years, New City has been a bastion of order in a fallen world. One crucial law has maintained the peace: it is illegal to place responsibility for the collapse of civilization on any one group. Anyone found guilty of Blaming is branded and stripped of citizenship.

But when some unwelcome visitors arrive from across the sea, old wounds break open, and no one is safe from Blame.

Available in electronic and print editions!

Emergency Transmission (Toxic World Book Four)

Trust is the only thing that can save the world.

The problem is, everyone has their own agenda.

When an offshore platform starts emitting toxic fumes that threaten to destroy the last outposts of civilization, the residents of New City have to team up with a foreign freighter to fix it. But a lingering mistrust remains, and neither side has the resources to stop the leak.

That is, until help comes from the least reliable source.

Can old enemies finally set aside their differences for the greater good?

Available in electronic and print editions!

Tales from the Toxic World

A scavenger with a wondrous artifact from the Old Times sets out to avenge his past ...

The sheriff of a post-apocalyptic shantytown investigates a baffling murder ...

Two fishermen in a toxic sea make a startling discovery ...

A peddler has to compromise his faith to help others and not end up dead ...

Here are nine stories from a grim future that's all too possible. The world has been destroyed by war, pollution, and environmental degradation. Now only a few lonely outposts struggle to keep the light of civilization lit amid vast toxic wasteland filled with human predators.

This collection is a long-awaited addition to the popular Toxic World post-apocalyptic science fiction series. It's sure to please fans and newcomers to the series alike.

Available in electronic and print editions!

The Scavenger (A Toxic World Novelette)

In a world shattered by war, pollution, and disease, a lone scavenger discovers a priceless relic from the Old Times.

The problem is, it's stuck in the middle of the worst wasteland he knows—a contaminated city inhabited by insane chem addicts and vengeful villagers. Only his wits, his gun, and an unlikely ally can get him out alive.

Set in the Toxic World series introduced in the novel *Radio Hope*, this 10,000-word story explores more of the dangers and personalities that make up a post-apocalyptic world that's all too possible.

Available in electronic and print editions!

A Fine Likeness (House Divided Book One)

A Confederate guerrilla and a Union captain discover there's something more dangerous in the woods than each other.

Jimmy Rawlins is a teenage bushwhacker who leads his friends on ambushes of Union patrols. They join infamous guerrilla leader Bloody Bill Anderson on a raid through Missouri, but Jimmy questions his commitment to the cause when he discovers this madman plans to sacrifice a Union prisoner in a hellish ritual to raise the Confederate dead.

Richard Addison is an aging captain of a lackluster Union militia. Depressed over his son's death in battle, a glimpse of Jimmy changes his life. Jimmy and his son look so much alike that Addison becomes obsessed with saving him from Bloody Bill. Captain Addison must wreck his reputation to win this war within a war, while Jimmy must decide whether to betray the Confederacy to stop the evil arising in the woods of Missouri.

Available in print and electronic editions!

The River of Desperation (House Divided Book Two)
In the waning days of the Civil War, a secret conflict still rages...
Lieutenant Allen Addison of the *USS Essex* is looking forward to the South's defeat so he can build the life he's always wanted. Love and a promising business await him in St. Louis, but he is swept up in a primeval war between the forces of Order and Chaos, a struggle he doesn't understand and can barely believe in. Soon he is fighting to keep a grip on his sanity as he tries to save St. Louis from destruction.

The long-awaited sequel to *A Fine Likeness* continues the story of two opposing forces that threaten to tear the world apart.

Available in electronic and print editions!

The Last Hotel Room
He came to Tangier to die, but life isn't done with him yet.
Tom Miller has lost his job, his wife, and his dreams. Broke and alone, he ends up in a flophouse in Morocco, ready to end it all. But soon he finds himself tangled in a web of danger and duty as he's pulled into scamming tourists for a crooked cop while trying to help a Syrian

refugee boy survive life on the streets. Can a lifelong loser do something good for a change?

A portion of my royalties will go to a charity for Syrian refugees.

Available in electronic and print editions!

The Night the Nazis Came to Dinner and Other Dark Tales

A spectral dinner party goes horribly wrong...

An immortal warrior hopes a final battle will set him free...

A big-game hunter preys on endangered species to supply an illicit restaurant...

A new technology soothes First World guilt...

Here are four dark tales that straddle the boundary between reality and speculation. You better hope they don't come true.

Available in electronic edition!

The Quintessence of Absence

Can a drug-addicted sorcerer sober up long enough to save a kidnapped girl and his own duchy?

In an alternate eighteenth-century Germany where magic is real and paganism never died, Lothar is in the bonds of nepenthe, a powerful drug that gives him ecstatic visions. It has also taken his job, his friends, and his self-respect. Now his old employer has rehired Lothar to find the man's daughter, who is in the grip of her own addiction to nepenthe.

As Lothar digs deeper into the girl's disappearance, he uncovers a plot that threatens the entire Duchy of Anhalt, and finds that the only way to stop it is to face his own weakness.

Available in electronic edition!

Writing Books by Sean McLachlan

Writing Secrets of the World's Most Prolific Authors

What does it take to write 100 books? What about 500? Or 1,000?

That may sound like an impossibly high number, but it isn't. Some of the world's most successful authors wrote hundreds of books over the course of highly lucrative careers. Isaac Asimov wrote more than 300 books. Enid Blyton wrote more than 800. Legendary Western writer Lauren Bosworth Paine wrote close to 1,000.

Some wrote even more.

This book examines the techniques and daily habits of more than a dozen of these remarkable writers to show how anyone with the right mindset can massively increase their word count without sacrificing quality. Learn the secrets of working on several projects simultaneously, of reducing the time needed for each book, and how to build the work ethic you need to become more prolific than you ever thought possible.

Available in electronic and print edition!

History Books by Sean McLachlan

Wild West History
Apache Warrior vs. US Cavalryman: 1846-86 (Osprey: 2016)
Tombstone—Wyatt Earp, the O.K. Corral, and the Vendetta Ride
(Osprey: 2013)
The Last Ride of the James-Younger Gang (Osprey: 2012)
Civil War History
Ride Around Missouri: Shelby's Great Raid 1863 (Osprey: 2011)
American Civil War Guerrilla Tactics (Osprey: 2009)
Missouri History
Outlaw Tales of Missouri (Globe Pequot: 2009)
Missouri: An Illustrated History (Hippocrene: 2008)
It Happened in Missouri (Globe Pequot: 2007)
Medieval History
Medieval Handgonnes: The First Black Powder Infantry Weapons
(Osprey: 2010)
Byzantium: An Illustrated History (Hippocrene: 2004)
African History
Armies of the Adowa Campaign 1896: The Italian Disaster in
Ethiopia (Osprey: 2011)